Repent at Leisure

By

Stevie Turner

Repent at Leisure

Copyright Stevie Turner 2015

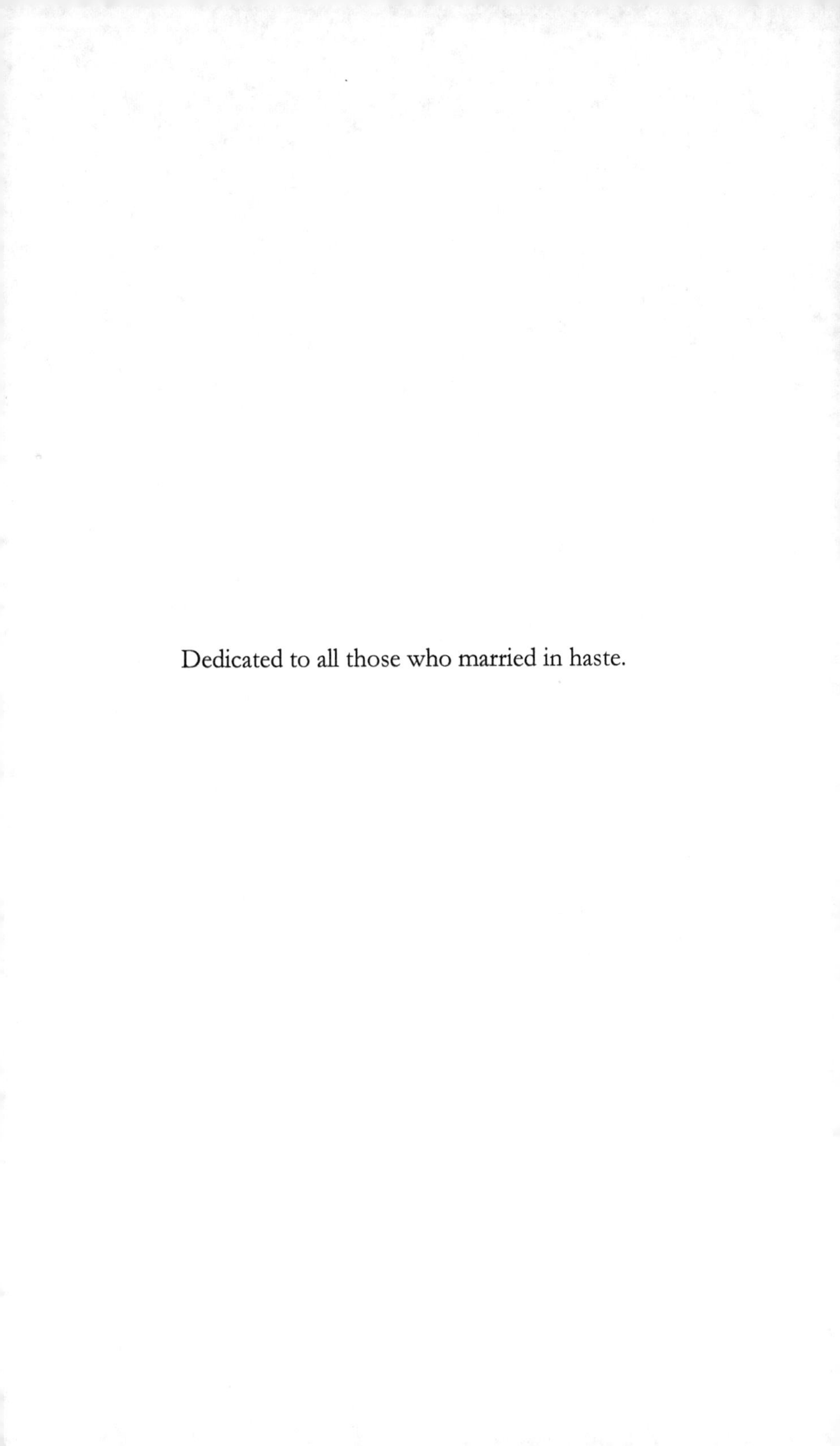

Dedicated to all those who married in haste.

SYNOPSIS

Paul McAdam wakes up to the sight of a strange girl in his bed. He has no idea who she is or where she has come from. Cat Taylor worms her way into Paul's life, eventually moving into his Edinburgh flat. However, the arrangement suits Paul quite well until he meets Anita Fairfax, the love of his life and the girl he wishes to marry. Cat has to go, but Paul finds that she is not very interested in moving out.

When Cat is found dead in Paul's flat, the police are suspicious of Paul even though there is not a shred of evidence to incriminate him. Anita is in love with Paul and agrees to marry him, glossing over the fact that Paul is an angry young man and prone to violent outbursts of temper. Anita is sure that her love for Paul will change him for the better, but after they are married and Paul's anger becomes more of a problem, she begins to wonder whether her new husband could have been Cat's killer all along…..

Table of Contents

CHAPTER 1...1
CHAPTER 2...7
CHAPTER 3... 13
CHAPTER 4... 19
CHAPTER 5... 25
CHAPTER 6... 33
CHAPTER 7... 41
CHAPTER 8... 47
CHAPTER 9... 53
CHAPTER 10 59
CHAPTER 11 63
CHAPTER 12 69
CHAPTER 13 77
CHAPTER 14 83
CHAPTER 15 87
CHAPTER 16 93
CHAPTER 17 101
CHAPTER 18 109
CHAPTER 19 117
CHAPTER 20 121
CHAPTER 21 129
CHAPTER 22 135
CHAPTER 23 145
CHAPTER 24 151
CHAPTER 25 157
CHAPTER 26 163
CHAPTER 27 169
CHAPTER 28 175
CHAPTER 29 181
CHAPTER 30 187
CHAPTER 31 193
CHAPTER 32 199
CHAPTER 33 205
CHAPTER 34 213

CHAPTER 35 219
CHAPTER 36 223
CHAPTER 37 233
CHAPTER 38 237
CHAPTER 39 241
CHAPTER 40 247
CHAPTER 41 253
CHAPTER 42 263
CHAPTER 43 269
CHAPTER 44 275

PART 1 - PAUL
CHAPTER 1
JANUARY 1ST 2000

DARREN MUST HAVE spiked my bloody drink again; I'll kill the bastard.

I sit up in bed, rub my eyes and give her the once over as I inch back the covers. She's naked and reasonably good-looking, but the blonde hair doesn't quite reach the roots and the face is caked in make-up. I've always liked the natural look, so God knows why I went and picked *her*. Perhaps I didn't; probably Darren gave her a good time and then lumbered me with her after I'd passed out.

My mouth's as dry as a badger's chuff, and my head is throbbing. I need some coffee. Whoever she is sleeps on as I climb out of bed and slide into some jeans. As I open the bedroom door I can see Darren, fully clothed and dead to the world on the settee. We must have had a fucking ace time of it last night; if only I could remember.

The noise of the kettle brings Darren out of his stupor. As he comes into the kitchen his mullet's awry like he's got a surfboard on his head. Yawning, I reach for two mugs from the cupboard and heap a spoonful of coffee in each. I indicate with a thumb over in the direction of the bedroom.

"Who's the bird?"

Darren hacks up enough tar to fill all the potholes along the M1.

"You're asking me? You're the one who was with her all night."

"Yeah, but *some* bastard spiked my drinks."

My look of venom informs him in no uncertain terms whom I suspect of perpetrating the crime. Darren, innocence personified, shrugs his shoulders, picks up the kettle, and pours boiling water into the mugs.

"Nothin' to do with me, mate."

"Yeah, and my dick's two foot long."

"You should be so lucky." Darren adds coffee to an extra mug. "Here; give her one."

"I already did, didn't I?" I sigh.

"Possibly; you were going at it hammer and tongs in there last night."

"Shit."

The girl stumbles out into the living area wearing *my* shirt.

"Coffee; great." She takes a steaming mug from the worktop. "Any sugar?"

"You're sweet enough, darlin'" Darren eyes her up and down.

"I forgot to buy any." I mumble.

"I'll pop out and get some later." The girl settles herself down in my armchair, takes small sips from the mug, and puts her feet up on the coffee table.

Did she think she was staying then? I swallow a wave of irritation at her proprietary air, and wish both of them would piss off and leave me alone to rattle around my flat in peace and recover in my own time from the previous night's excesses.

"That won't be necessary. Look; I've got relatives visiting this afternoon. I assume the two of you have got homes to go to?"

I hope I sound convincing enough. Darren nods as he drains the last of his coffee and looks at the girl.

"It's already the afternoon, but hey, I'm gone. D'you want a lift, darlin'?"

"The name's Cat, and I'm *not* your darling."

The girl gives him the evil eye. By this time I don't care *whose* darling she is, just so long as she isn't mine.

"You'll pay a fortune for a taxi on New Year's Day." Darren smooths down his mullet with one hand and searches for his car keys with the other. "Last chance for a lift. Where do you live?"

"Abercrombie Road, but Paul can take me home later." I must have told her my name at some point, although I have no recollection of ever doing so. I try to mask a rising fury as I look at her.

"I'm low on petrol, and there won't be any garages open today. Wherever Abercrombie Road is, you'll have to walk if you don't go with Darren now."

"*Okay, okay.*" She exhales with venom and jumps up. "It's nice to be wanted, I must say."

Fuck off! The drums in my head start playing that Cozy Powell song that I can never remember the name of. She goes back into the bedroom and emerges wearing a tight red mini-dress, a black jacket, and black stilettos.

"I can't find my mobile phone, so I'll give you a chance to find it and I'll come back tomorrow."

"Aye."

Yeah, whatever. Just go.

"See you later, mate."

I nod to Darren as he ushers the girl out of the door. I suddenly feel decidedly sick, and only just about make it to the toilet before violently upchucking the coffee and whatever else is festering in my stomach from the night before. After rinsing my mouth I stumble back to bed and am asleep almost as soon as my head touches the pillow.

When I wake up again the flat is in darkness. I check the digital clock, which shows 6:08 pm. I can still smell the girl's cloying, musky perfume on the sheets, which only adds to my foul mood. With one fluid motion I turn on the lamp, climb out of bed, and then unhinge the duvet from its cover. After ripping off the fitted sheet and pillowcases and stuffing them into the washing machine with the duvet cover I feel somewhat calmer. I add more soap powder than usual in an effort to rid myself of any trace of my night-time companion, and hit the shower with more eagerness than usual. After towelling myself dry I look at my reflection in the mirror; reddish-brown hair in need of a cut, atop a pale, washed out face featuring the sharp Campbell nose inherited from my mother's side of the family, and tired-looking brown eyes.

"Happy New Year." I say out loud to myself. "You're a real horse's arse."

After a light supper I take my bedclothes out of the tumble drier and find the phone that Cat (or was it Kate?) must have hidden, pushed down between the mattress and the wall as I re-make the bed. How the fuck would a phone that size get *there* unless somebody had placed it in that exact spot on purpose? I wrack my brain again and again to try and remember any vestige of the night before, but give up in the end and hoped to God I'd used a condom. I scour the carpet for evidence of any used johnnies to no avail, and check the state of the old chap lying still and quiescent inside my jogging bottoms. Thankfully, as far as I can see, it seems devoid of any nasty little rashes; *so far, so good.*

The great thing about living in Edinburgh and being born on the thirty first of December is that Darren and I can always celebrate my birthday in style on New Year's Eve, and can get pissed in peace without it being in the back of our minds that we have to get up early the next morning and go to work. This year is no exception. It has taken me most of the day to feel human again, but now at last I have managed to reach twenty-one, the age of maturity, which coincided nicely with much end-of-century celebrating. I have the key to the door, but actually, if truth be told, that particular door has been well and truly open for at least two years already.

It's close to nine thirty that same night when I hear the doorbell ringing. I find it hard to mask my disappointment at the sight of my latest bed companion standing there.

"Hi." I yawn.

"Try and control your excitement at the sight of me."

The girl shoots me an evil stare, and I wish she would just go away.

"I'll give it a go." I nod.

"I've come for my phone." She looks past me into the hallway.

I have anticipated her visit. I reach behind me and pick

the phone up from its resting place on the hall

table. "Here you are."

She takes the phone from me and puts it in her handbag. "Aren't you going to invite me in?" "What for?"

"Coffee."

"I wasn't planning on it." I sigh.

"Can I just do a wee then? I'm desperate."

"Be quick then, 'cos I'm going to bed."

She steps into the hallway and takes off her coat. Apart from fishnet stockings and black stilettos I cannot help but notice that she's wearing nothing underneath.

The old boy stands up stiffer than a March gale. It's going to be a long night.

CHAPTER 2

"WHO THE FUCK do you think I am? I'm Paul *McAdam*, not Paul Getty!"

I stare at half of a cow lying on my plate. Cat chews a chip thoughtfully and then gives me a smile.

"Don't worry; I paid for it."

"What with? Shirt buttons? Fillet steak isn't cheap, you know."

"I've got money. You've got to keep your strength up."

She pouts with those red luscious lips of hers, and I feel one of her feet exploring my groin under the table. I've tried to resist the insidious way in which she's been worming herself into my flat and my life for three months, but what bloke can say no if it's handed to him on a plate (the sex, I mean, not the steak)? I look down at the feast in front of me.

"How come your dole money stretches this far then?"

"It doesn't."

"So who's making up the shortfall?" I spear a tender piece of steak with my fork.

"Mind your own business."

I idly wonder if she's on the game, but then again she's never out of my flat. I must admit the place has never looked so clean and tidy, and after a day at work spent slaving over a hot computer it's nice that dinner's ready when I get in, but actually at the moment what I would really prefer instead of a wife is a personal maid. I'm only 21, and not ready to settle down and do the pipe and slippers thing yet.

It's pay day, and Darren owes me a pint. We get paid weekly at Dodd's Computers, and so I take him up on his offer before he's skint and asking me for money again as usual. I leave Cat at home complaining at having to spend the evening on her own.

"It'll be boring; there's nothing on telly tonight." She sighs as she sits on the settee with her feet up on my coffee table and channel-hops with the remote control.

I want to spend a night out with my mate. There's nothing wrong with that, and so I let her know how it is.

"It's boys only. We'll be talking about bikes, birds and beer."

"As long as that's all you'll be doing."

What is it with birds that as soon as they get their feet under your table they want to take over your life? I didn't even go out looking for Cat; she found me, just like her feline namesake. Feed them and they're yours. I don't know where she came from, but suddenly she's living in my flat and starting to dictate what I should or shouldn't be doing in my own spare time. This whole thing's gone arse about tit.

"Look; if a bird talks to me in the pub I'm not going to ignore her, am I?"

"But you're with me now." Cat whines, puts down the remote, and looks up at me from the settee.

We're not joined at the hip. Give it a rest; it's just a blokes' night out."

Darren's already got the first round in as I walk through the doors of The Rat and Pigeon.

"Cheers mate." I take a long glug of ale. "I needed that."

"What's up?" Darren looks at me with interest.

"Bloody Cat." I shake my head. "I think she wants my babies; the whole marriage thing. I don't want to spend the rest of my life with her; I'm suffocating." I drain the rest of the pint in one go.

"Christ, you've only known her a few weeks."

"Yeah." I nod. "I'm going to give her the elbow; I can't stand it." I sigh.

"Take her out somewhere public where she won't make a scene." Darren advises, now sporting a frothy Guinness moustache. "I had to do that with Jane."

"How did she take it?" I enquire grimly.

"She walked out of the restaurant and left me sitting there like a prize prat, but the deed was done, so to speak."

"Cat's cleaning round all the time; hoovering, dusting, polishing and cooking." I roll my eyes skywards before adding an afterthought. "The sex is great though."

"Fuck! What are you complaining about then?" Darren bursts out laughing.

"It's not funny." I look morosely into the bottom of my empty glass. "I'll look round in a minute and I'll have six kids in tow."

The door opens and I watch Miss Perfect appear again, with a couple of other girls; this time wearing pale pink. I've seen her at the bar a few times recently, and I find it difficult to take my eyes off the blonde hair cascading down to her waist; it shines and shimmies and seems to move under the pub's spotlights with a life of its own. Darren follows my line of vision and gives me a smirk.

"Forget it; she's way out of your league."

"A bloke can dream, can't he?" I pick up my glass. "It's my round; another Guinness?"

"Yeah, ta."

At the bar I make sure I'm standing as near to the vision of loveliness as I can, without intruding into her personal space and risking a bollocking. I turn to face her and contort my features into a kind of grimace that I hope passes for a smile.

"Can I buy you a drink?"

One of the girls she's with sniggers, and I find myself blushing furiously. I almost never blush, and I could stab myself in the arm with fury. The girl is obviously finding my predicament amusing, but doesn't really say anything in reply. Embarrassed beyond measure I slink back to Darren with two pints of the black stuff.

"I'll never understand women." I thump two glasses down with more force than necessary. "Fucking lezzies, the lot of them."

"I take it she turned you down then?" Darren's mouth is trying not to turn up at the corners.

"Didn't even bother replying."

"Oh well; you've still got Cat to go home
to." "Oh Christ."

I feel like getting well and truly leathered. Everything in my life is going Pete Tong.

Luckily I feel somewhat happier after the third pint. Darren goes off to point Percy at the porcelain, but while I sit alone at the table wondering whether to suggest a kebab or a curry, I feel a light tap on my shoulder. Looking up I fall into the blonde bombshell's iridescent grey eyes and the world stops turning for a moment. She leans over me and her low-cut t-shirt sags forward, exposing the top of a pink bra.

"Sorry about my cousins; they're so crass. You *can* buy me a drink sometime if you like."

I'm not sure if I've heard her right, and for a moment I'm actually stumped for words.

"Er….tomorrow?" My mouth is hanging open as wide as the entrance to the St. Leonard's tunnel. "See you
here about eight then." "Oh…w-what's your
name?" I manage to stutter. "Anita Fairfax.
Yours?"
"Paul. Paul McAdam."

She smiles, then turns to go back to her cousins leaving me gobsmacked and dazed, effects not altogether due to two pints of Guinness and one pint of bitter, but I would say more so to the sight of Anita's agreeable cleavage, slim figure, and long legs.

CHAPTER 3

AS I LEAVE the office I decide I'm going to be what they call 'fashionably late' to the pub; it's no good appearing too eager. However, first I've got the problem of convincing Cat that I've got to work late. I'm getting a bit pissed off with all this intrusion into my freedom; it's getting so that she wants to know where I'm going to be every hour of every frigging day. It's got to stop.

In the privacy of the car I check my phone, ignore the text message from Cat, and call home. She answers straight away.

"Where are you?"

"Gotta work late."

"Why?"

She sounds cheesed off. Well, so am I.

"A customer in the US has a software issue. I've got to call him and take over his screen and try to sort it out. He's only available from three o'clock his time, and that's eight o'clock our time. I'm going to have to read the software manual for a couple of hours beforehand as well, although in the end it'll probably be down to the biological interface."

"Eh?"

She sounds puzzled and astounded at my technical know-how, but I decide to let her down gently.

"Finger trouble."

I surprise myself with the plausibility of the excuse. Cat falls for it like a shot.

"Oh; well okay. You can warm your dinner up in the microwave when you get back."

"Ta." I breathe a sigh of relief. "What have you got planned for this evening then?"

I don't really care what she's doing, as long as she's not doing it with me. I listen with half an ear while thinking about having sex with Anita Fairfax.

"I think I'll go down The Riot House with Kerry."

"Have fun."

"Yeah; see you later then."

"Okay."

I turn off the phone, pleased at having got away with it. I start the car and head off to Darren's bedsit; I can have a wash and shave there.

Anita's either arrived, seen I'm not there and gone, or is hanging it out even longer than I am for the full effect. I check my phone; it's twenty to nine. The pub is about half full. I order myself a pint and sit facing the door, and curse my right leg as it twitches with nerves.

I'm about to give up at five past nine and go home, when she swans in like the Queen of Sheba. Every bloke's head swivels in her direction, and I feel like some sort of prince amongst paupers as she strides purposely towards me and tosses her hair.

"Sorry I'm late. Have you been waiting long?"

I drown in her perfume and manage to mask my irritation at her tardiness quite well.

"Nah; only just got here."

"Oh good."

She settles herself down opposite me at the table, and looks hopefully in the direction of the bar. I stand up and pull out my wallet.

"What'll I get you to drink?"

"Hmm….Pimms and lemonade please."

She gives me a smile that makes me feel weak at the knees, I suddenly don't give a rat's arse that she's an hour late. I strut up to the bar like I own the place and give the landlord a knowing wink.

"Alright Ray? One Pimms and lemonade please, and one pint of bitter."

Ray snorts with contempt as he serves the drinks.

"You can have a lemonade without the Pimms, or they'll have my licence, and I know her dad, Mike Fairfax; he'll have my balls. Anita's a cracker though, you lucky bugger!"

"It's my charm; they all fall for it in the end."

"Fuck off." Ray chuckles as I hand him the money.

She sits demurely, ignoring obvious glances in her direction. I stride back to the table and sit opposite her, trying to block out stares from the mostly male clientele.

"I've only seen you here very recently." I pass a glass to her. "Have you just moved to the area?"

"No; I'm up here from London, visiting my dad and stepmother, and various other relatives. I come up quite often though."

I feel a sudden stab of disappointment that she lives 400

miles away. Her southern accent is music to my ears, and as she crosses her legs and takes a sip of her drink I start to sweat as I try and think of something to say.

"Do you work in London?"

I cringe. My question sounds utterly banal. However, I'm unprepared for the answer.

"Yes, I'm an actress. How about you?"

She catches me off guard and I don't know whether to take her seriously, so I play her at her own game.

"I'm an airline pilot."

"Really?" Her eyes twinkle before she gives me a quizzical look. "Aren't you a little young?"

"I'm twenty one and an aerodynamic genius. Long haul to Australia tomorrow, so make the most of me tonight."

She eyes my pint with suspicion.

"I thought pilots weren't supposed to drink before a flight?"

"This one does." I pour a good half pint of bitter down my throat in one go.

"Thank goodness I'm not getting on *your* plane then."

I'm suddenly enjoying the banter, and relax a bit more and stop sweating.

"So what do you really do for a living?" I fix her with one of my looks that sends Cat into squeals of joy.

"I'm seventeen, eighteen in August though, but still at college actually." She appears sheepish at the revelation. "I'm studying performing arts, but saying I'm an actress sounds better."

She's younger than I thought; Ray was right. I'll have to tread carefully with this one.

"Oh, well never mind." I shrug. "I'm not an airline pilot either."

"I figured that." She laughs. "Where do you really work then?"

"I'm a technical support guy for a computer software company here in Edinburgh, but saying I'm an airline pilot sounds better."

We both burst out laughing, and I find I'm enjoying her company immensely. I suddenly want her to stay with me for the rest of my life.

"How long are you up here for?" I venture the question that I don't really want to ask.

"Another few days. I'm just here for the Easter holidays. College starts again next week." She nods. "And I'm learning how to drive. Dad says that if I pass my test he'll buy me a car."

"Lucky old you." I sigh. "My dad always pissed his money up the wall."

"What d'you mean?"

She appears puzzled. She has a delightfully innocent air about her which clashes somewhat vividly with her outward appearance. I kick myself for the past tense *faux pas*.

"He drank it all away."

"Are all Scotsmen alcoholics?" Her eyes twinkle again.

"He was; I'm not." I grin at her. "But I'm working on it."

When last orders are sounded I'm disappointed that the evening's come to an end. We've spent all evening chatting and I've only drunk two pints of bitter as well, which Darren would rib me about if he knew.

"Can I see you tomorrow?" I clutch at a straw of hope.

"Yeah, if you like. My dad will be waiting outside in the

car now, so I'd better go."

She stands up and I want to punch the air with happiness.

"Same time, same place tomorrow then?" I venture as I help her on with her coat.

"Okay."

I'm so buoyed up I don't know whether to kiss her or not. I look past her and it seems all the blokes and even Ray are looking in my direction waiting to find out. In the end I decide against it and let her go.

CHAPTER 4

CAT'S STILL UP and is watching TV when I get home. I don't know why I've let our non-relationship progress so far. Tonight I found the woman I want to spend the rest of my life with, and unfortunately it's not the one who's now got her arms around my neck.

"Hi." She kisses me. "Have you been in the pub?"

"I had a swift half with Darren after work." I'm an expert on lying by now. "I'll need to work a couple more late nights, but everything should be back to normal by next week."

I fervently hope so. Normal to me means only one occupant in my flat, and having the bed to myself. I've just got to find the right way of getting what I want. Cat nibbles my neck and rubs herself against me.

"I've booked us a little holiday today. Two weeks in Menorca. Book the last two weeks off in July when you get to the office tomorrow."

"What?" Astounded, I hold her at arm's length. "Who's paid for it?"

"I have." Cat smiles. "Don't worry; you won't need to splash out for a thing."

"You might have discussed it with me first!" I feel righteous indignation at the increasing loss of control over my life. "And where the hell have you found the money for a Spanish holiday?"

"I told you before; it's none of your business." Cat smiles mysteriously as she unzips my jeans. "Perhaps you can show me just how grateful you are that I'm looking after you so well."

Do I want to go to Menorca? You bet I do, but with Anita instead. However, the deed is done now and I can't get out of it. I am determined to end the relationship after the holiday though. Up until then I'll have to put up with having sex with Cat while imagining I'm making love to Anita. Who knows, I might even be able to manage to superimpose Anita's face onto Cat's right at the crucial moment. It's a tough job, but hey, somebody's got to do it.

Tonight I'm right on time, and surprisingly so is she. A chap who I assume is Anita's father drives up to the pub just as I arrive, and I can see him giving me the once over as she opens the passenger door. I decide to put his mind at ease. I smile at Anita who looks ravishing in her jeans and a yellow top, and then bend down and peer in at a sandy-haired man aged about forty sitting in the driver's seat wearing rimless glasses, who is dressed casually in corduroys and a long-sleeved shirt. He's tapping his wedding ring against the steering wheel in time with a song playing on the radio.

"Hi; I'm Paul McAdam." I hold out my right hand towards him as he sits there in the car.

"Pleased to meet you." The chap clasps my hand with his own. "I'm Mike Fairfax, Anita's dad."

The handshake is firm, and even better is the fact that he doesn't look as though he's going to get out and punch me on the nose. He doesn't seem too bad at all really, and I feel a little glow of acceptance.

"I'll be back for Anita at half past ten." Mike Fairfax gets his message across with a smile.

"Absolutely." I nod inanely. "We'll be here."

As we make our way into the pub, Anita grins at me.

"Sorry about Dad; he's a bit over- protective."

"And so he should be." I nod. "It's what dads are for."

"At home Mum lets me do my own thing, but Dad can be a bit of a pain."

"You're only seventeen; he's looking out for you. Did your mum re-marry?"

"No; there's just the two of us at home." Anita sits down at the table we had vacated the previous evening. "Mum and Dad divorced when I was seven. Dad married his secretary and Mum's got a boyfriend, but says she never wants to get married again."

"Oh, sorry." I grimace. "My dad buggered off years ago. Can't say I was upset about it at the time though; all they ever did was argue. I've got a brother, Terry, but he lives in Australia. What're you drinking by the way?"

She gives a little tinkly laugh, and looks up at me.

"Just a coke please. The barman knows my dad, so it's no secret I'm underage. I think that may be why he keeps on staring at me."

"That's because he's a randy bugger and you're looking good enough to eat."

"Leave it out." She blushes but appears pleased.

It's a relief sometimes not to have to keep up with Darren in the drinking stakes. I even order an orange juice to Ray's surprise, and Anita and I sit there ignoring all the other punters and looking at each other through rose-tinted glasses. I am more relaxed than I've been in a long time, and want to find out everything about her.

"So, what's your college course like?"

"It's great; we're doing acting, singing, dancing, and choreography. I want to be one of those dancers you see in the London West End shows."

"Great." I nod, not able to take my eyes off her. "I'm sure it'll happen for you. You've just got to believe in yourself."

"Mum's got a few contacts in the business. She used to do modelling." She takes a sip of her drink and gives me her full attention. "What's your job like? Do you like it better than flying planes?"

I roll my eyes and laugh.

"Er…sorry about that. Yeah, I did computer studies at college. I work for Dodd's Computers. The job's okay; I just help people out who can't be bothered or who are too thick to understand software manuals."

"Like me." She chuckles.

"No, not like you. I've found out that quite a lot of people don't want to read about how to set things up. If they've bought one of our computers they want somebody to show them; and that's where I come in. They come into the office and I go through it all with them, or sometimes I sort it out over the internet or on the phone."

"So you're one of those I.T nerds then." Anita giggles.

"If you like, yeah. I've left my pebble specs at home though, so I might bump into the furniture."

She has an infectious laugh. The orange juice is sitting like concrete in my stomach, and suddenly I want her all to myself.

"Fancy a walk in the park? It's just across the road."

"Sure." She finishes her coke, stands up, and puts on her jacket. "I'll just nip to the loo first."

I stand outside and wait for her. I'm walking on air. I don't even want to get inside her pants at this stage. Well, I do, but I don't care if it takes the rest of my time on earth to be able to do so. Is this love? I think it might be.

She links her arm through mine as we cross the road to the park, and I feel like the king of the world. I want the evening to last forever. There's a football match taking place on the floodlit astro-turf. I recognise some of the players, and I want them to see Anita. We sit on a bench near the pitch and watch the match. She shivers and snuggles up closer.

"I'm cold."

Her thin jacket is impractical for a Scottish April evening. I venture an arm around her shoulders, and to my surprise she doesn't resist. I don't care if my arse freezes over, I'm happy to sit here all night just so long as she's with me. My mates give us a few glances, my fingers turn blue, and my heart's fit to burst with joy.

When the match is over I realise I can hardly feel my hands at all, and it occurs to me that we could both be suffering from early hypothermia.

"Shall we go back to the pub for a wee dram before your dad turns up?"

Anita can only nod.   A wonderful wall of heat greets us

as we head into the Rat and Pigeon, and I slip Ray a fiver for a couple of whiskies. He shakes his head in Anita's direction, and comes back with one whisky, one ginger ale, and some change. Returning to the table, I keep my back to him, mix the contents of both glasses together, and pour half of it back into her glass.

"Here; drink this. It'll warm you up."

She quaffs it back in an instant, coughing as the whisky touches the back of her throat, and the colour comes back into her cheeks. I take both of her hands and hold them between mine.

"I'm going to miss you when you go back to London."

"I'll miss you too." She sniffs. "My nose is running."

"Lovely; thanks for sharing that information."

"My pleasure." She giggles and then her face falls. "Dad's driving me back the day after tomorrow."

"Can I see you again before you go home?" I give her fingers a squeeze.

"Yes, I'd like that."

"Here; write down your email address if you've got a pen in your bag." I hand her my beermat. "And your mobile number. I'll see you here again tomorrow night at seven if you like."

"Okay."

She gives me a dazzling smile that makes my toes curl as she returns the beermat. I pocket the information carefully, then lean forward and plant a quick kiss on her lips. There is definitely a favourable response, and I somehow know that tomorrow evening's going to be a good one.

CHAPTER 5

REALITY SETS IN as I walk back to Cat. I've no idea how to extricate myself from the honey trap that I've let myself fall into. Her love is leech-like; my lifeblood is slowly but surely being sucked away while Cat bloats and gloats with contentment. I shake my head as I walk. Something needs to be done, and *fast*.

She's standing there in the hallway as I open the front door. This time she's naked except for a black leather basque, suspenders, black stockings and stilettos. Surprisingly, and not for the first time either, I find that nothing's happening to the old John Thomas down below. I sigh.

"You'll catch cold walking around like that."

"Ah, but you love it really."

She presses her body against mine, and I swear she's purring. However, I've just met the girl I'm going to marry, and it's not the one who's now wrapping one foot around the back of my left leg.

"Leave it out; I'm knackered."

"All work and no play makes Paul a dull boy."

Her tongue eases its way into my right ear canal, and

unfortunately for me the experience is less than favourable. It's eleven o'clock at night and all I want to do is go to bed and dream about Anita.

"Fancy a cup of tea?"

I push her away. Pouting, she untangles her limbs from mine.

"I fancy a bit more than that. I've been sitting here all night waiting for you to come home."

"Cat, I need to talk to you."

I make my way to the kitchen and switch on the kettle. She follows me in.

"What's up?"

She leans back against the worktop in her underwear, sultry and smouldering. At this precise moment in time most blokes would have followed their primal instincts and done something else instead of making tea, but as it happens making tea is all I feel like doing.

"I can't see a future for us, Cat."

I stir in some sugar lumps and wait for the fall-out. "What d'you mean?"

"Exactly what I say. I want to end our relationship."

"Why? What have I done? I thought we were getting along great?"

Cat looks ready to cry, and I feel a complete prick for leading her on. I shrug and look down on the ground.

"It's like this; I've found somebody else."

I hear a sharp intake of breath and the stilettos clicking a tattoo on the lino as she stomps around to face me.

"You bastard! So you haven't been at work all evening then?"

I shake my head and look up at her.

"No."

The resulting slap is not altogether unexpected. What I do not foresee is the blubbering wreck my temptress dissolves into in just one brief nanosecond. I've never been any good with wailing women, and this one is no exception.

"I've got nowhere else to go!" Her tears suddenly began to fall like driving rain as she flings herself at me.

"Where did you live before?" I put the cup down before I spill tea down the front of her basque.

"With a boyfriend", she sobbed, "But he chucked me out too!"

"Well there's no hurry to move out. Leave it until you've found somewhere to rent."

I sigh and put my arms around her, she stops crying in an instant, and like the late Princess Diana I begin to wonder if there's going to be three of us in any future marriage.

Cat's still asleep when the alarm wakes me up at six thirty. I slide out of bed and make for the bathroom to get washed and shaved. There's no sound from the bedroom as I grab my car keys and open the front door.

Before I start the engine I check my phone. A message from Anita has popped up.

'Morning! Don't tell me…… you're on a plane and can't explain!'

Do you ever wish you could take back something you said? What the fuck was I thinking of when I told her I was an airline pilot? She's never going to let me live it down. It's too early for me to think of a suitable response, and so I just type in a short text.

'Still on for tonight?'

The phone buzzes as I pull away from the kerb. Looking around briefly to make sure no boys in blue are going to jump out from behind a bush, I slow down and read the one-word reply with a grin.

'Yep.'

I can't face going back to my flat after work, and so hide out at Darren's place, but when an old girlfriend turns up it doesn't take the brains of a rocket scientist to work out that I'm not wanted. I head straight to the pub at six thirty, but Anita's already waiting outside. I feel a small stab of pleasure at the sight of her.

"Hi! Are you early or am I late?" I give her a kiss and start to drown in her eyes.

"We're both early." She laughs and links her arm with mine. "Come on; let's take a walk. Dad's not coming back for me until half past ten."

I pull the collar of my jacket up in a futile effort to ward off the high wind chill factor.

"Where d'you want to go then?"

"Back to yours. It's nearby isn't it?"

I suffer one of those heartsink moments as silently as I can.

"Er…we could do, but you know how it is if a bloke lives on his own…..."

"That's okay. I don't mind."

What to do? To have Anita come face to face with Cat in her basque would be the end of a beautiful relationship.

The cogs in my head whirr at supersonic speed trying to think of an excuse.

"I haven't cleaned up. It's like a pigsty."

"I get the feeling you don't want me to see where you live."

Her tone is mocking, but her expression is serious. As I reluctantly agree to take her back to the flat, I hope and pray that Anita does not discover my 'flatmate'.

As we turn into Hayes Road I can see the flat is in darkness. As I turn my key in the lock, silence greets us as we step over the threshold. I switch on the hall light and quickly throw my jacket over Cat's pink hoodie hanging up on the hook.

"This is a nice place."

I watch Anita's head swivelling about, taking it all in. I have a quick think and consider the best place to take her would be the kitchen.

"Come and have a coffee. I'll put the kettle on."

As the fluorescent bulb splutters to life I start to relax a bit more. I notice that Anita's eyes are not missing a thing.

"I thought you said it was untidy? You keep it very neat and clean from what I can see."

I spoon de-caff coffee into two mugs and wait for the kettle to boil, feeling suddenly pleased with myself at thinking of an idea to win a few desperately-needed minutes to de-Cat the lounge.

"Tell you what; if you make the coffee I'll go around and pull the curtains."

"It's a deal."

I run off like a blue arse fly. I turn on the lamp in the front room, close the curtains, and snatch up one of Cat's bras which is draped over a chair, together with a woman's magazine on the coffee table. Looking around desperately as I hear footsteps coming up the hallway, I chuck them both underneath the settee and hope against hope there's no other incriminating evidence around.

"This is a lovely flat! Here's your coffee."

"Thanks."

I sit down nonchalantly on the settee, and try to slow my racing heart. Anita hands me a mug, and then snuggles up next to me.

"I don't want to go home tomorrow."

"I don't want you to either." I shake my head and sigh.

"I'll come up again in the summer holidays. We can keep in touch by phone until then."

"Can I have a kiss?" I find myself bursting with frustration and longing.

"I thought you'd never ask."

We put our mugs down on the table almost simultaneously and fall into each other's arms. I'm just about to blow a gasket when she whispers those four words that all blokes want to hear in a moment of crisis.

"I'm on the pill."

She could have knocked me down with a feather. There was I thinking she was as pure as the driven snow, only to find that one or even many sets of footprints had made it through the blizzard already to traverse that delightful and delectable route up the garden path.

I manage to mask my disappointment at not being first to reach the front door so to speak, and am just wondering how my exploration skills might compare with previous pathfinders, when she delivers the rest of her sentence as she takes off her panties.

"Mum put me on it for my acne. You're the first."

What can a bloke do when he's got two hours to spare and it's handed to him on a plate yet again? I rise to the occasion manfully, and with my own stalwart pole conquer the slippery terrain underfoot to eventually arrive with a gasp of joy at Nirvana.

At ten o'clock we still haven't got off the settee. We sit wrapped in each other's arms until I manage to get a quick look at my watch.

"Your dad will be waiting at the pub soon."

"Oh God!" She jumps up. "Where's your bathroom? I need to tidy myself up!"

We run as fast as we can do after two pleasurable hours of mutual exploration, and manage to get to the pub just as her dad is driving down the road. I give her a last kiss in the privacy of the pub's porch.

"Text me tomorrow when you get back to London."

"Will do. Paul…."

"What?"

"I think I love you."

I grinned at her.

"I *know* I love *you!*"

And with that she was gone.

I close my front door and lean back upon it with a sigh of happiness, and then retrieve Cat's bra and magazine from under the settee and make my way to the bathroom for a shower. Washed and dried, I pad naked towards the bedroom to find my pyjama shorts. As I open the bedroom door and switch on the light I see Cat, still wearing her basque, suspenders and stockings, lying spread-eagled on the bed with all four limbs manacled to the corner posts. A pillow obscures part of her face. As I lift the pillow I can see that her face is purple. Her body feels cold to my touch. She is very, very *dead*.

CHAPTER 6

I DON'T KNOW how long I stand there gazing at Cat. Yeah, I had wanted her out of my flat, but not like this. I feel sick to my stomach at the sight of her; all thoughts of the pleasant evening I've just spent are gone in a trice.

Within a short time my flat is swarming with police, forensics, and undertakers. Neighbours are trying to find out what's going on by peering in through the open front door, and one even gets as far as walking into the hallway and asks what's happening before I send him on his way with a couple of suitable words, the second one being *off*.

As I give a statement to the police I have the feeling that they don't really believe what I'm telling them. I am informed that investigations into Cat's death will begin, and that I will need to attend the station for questioning some time during the following day and possibly at other times in the future. The police take Darren and Anita's numbers to check out my alibi, and they inform me to leave the bedroom just as it is for the forensic guys.

With a sinking feeling of dismay I realise that apart from Darren whose bedsit I'd gone to straight after we'd finished work, the only other person who *can* give me an alibi is Anita, and our burgeoning relationship will probably be over before it starts when she finds out that I have been living with a hooker. Yes, the police inform me that from their past records Catherine Taylor was well known to them for soliciting around Edinburgh's red light district. So there was me, silly sod, wondering where all the money was coming from for holidays in Menorca and slabs of fillet steak, and all the time Cat had been on the game and using my flat as a knocking shop during the day while I was out. I had been taken in good and proper.

After the police have finished with me and the flat is empty, I bring some spare blankets and a pillow out of the airing cupboard and throw them on the settee. I'm glad I'm not allowed to sleep on the bed where Cat had died. Her body had been unbuckled from the manacles and put in the back of a private ambulance amidst scenes of great interest from the local rubberneckers. I feel like I've been putting on some sort of entertaining show for their convenience. I'm less than happy about spending the night on the settee where Anita and I had been so blissfully happy just a few short hours before, but I have no choice. As I try to get comfortable I inwardly sigh at the phone call I will need to make to Anita in the morning. I'm a coward as far as she's concerned and do not relish a confrontation to spoil our joy, and right now I can't bear to spoil the evening we've just had. As soon as she knows, her dad will then get his snout in the trough and I will be vilified into eternity and beyond, especially when he finds out what we'd been up to for the most part of the evening, and that I'm the one who's taken first bite of his daughter's cherry. I choose the denial route and close my eyes.

The dawn chorus outside is deafening. I wince with pain from the crick in my neck as I check the time; 05:47. Too early to call Anita. I stand up stiffly and hope the police don't decide to disturb her slumber too early.

I make myself some toast and grab a coffee, before inching open the bedroom door with my foot; whether it's some kind of ghoulish need to see inside, I don't know. The imprint of Cat's body on the duvet is still there, together with four handcuffs in the open position. I'm relieved though, that no blood is left on the duvet cover. As far as I can see there are no signs of a struggle.

Saddened, I turn away and head for the shower. By the time I'm dressed I can see I've missed two calls from Anita. I quickly find her number; it hardly rings at all before she's speaking ten to the dozen at me.

"The police have rung me. You bastard! You were going out with me but living with somebody else at the same time! My dad was right all along; he reckoned you were shifty, but I told him no! Now your girlfriend's dead and……!"

"Hold it; hold it!" I interject. "For a start Cat wasn't my girlfriend!"

"But she shared your bed?"

The tone of Anita's voice is with her increasing anger. I can tell that whatever I come up with as an explanation will go in one ear and out the other. I am well and truly *stuffed*.

"Let me explain….I love you!"

I want to cry at the situation I now find myself in. The girl of my dreams is rapidly fading to black, and more likely than not I'm going to receive a punch on the nose from her father if I meet them later on at the police station.

"Fuck off!"

The phone goes dead, and so does a part of me; the part

that had happily been inside the most beautiful girl in the world all yesterday evening. I decide there and then that if I can never make love with Anita again, then I really do not want sex with anybody else at all for the rest of my life. Nobody else will be good enough to make that dream of my own perfect, happy family come alive. I will have to just exist until I can make her come back to me.

She sits next to her father in the waiting room, and both glower at me as I announce myself to the duty sergeant on the desk. I feel like the criminal they all suspect me to be as I stand there and try to blend into the wallpaper.

"Hello Anita."

I turn towards her as she simultaneously shifts her gaze to the floor. Her expression is dour; my luck is out. Mike Fairfax stands up, steps forward, and blocks my view of his daughter.

"I'm driving Anita back to London after the interview."

My back is up. I think I've been given a death sentence without the aid of a trial, a defence lawyer, or a jury. "I'd

like to be given the chance to explain please."

My voice sounds shaky with anger. Mike Fairfax moves in closer.

"You will do in a minute." He indicates with his thumb that somebody is coming towards us. "And I for one can't wait to hear it."

I'm seated in the interview room as far away from Anita as Mike Fairfax and DC Elliott can manage. I sit at one end of an oblong table and look down its length to the girl I want to marry, who keeps her eyes fixed on a cup of coffee in front of her. DC Elliott sighs, stares at me, and picks up a pen.

"Let's hear it then."

Whatever I say I realise that probably nobody's ever going to believe me. I'm hung, drawn and quartered before I even start.

"One morning I woke up and Catherine Taylor was in my bed. I have no recollection of how she got there."

There's a snort of disbelief from Mike Fairfax. Anita's expression remains impassive. DC Elliott looks up with interest from his notebook.

"When was this?"

"A few months' ago. It seems she had nowhere else to go; I sort of took her in. She never really left my flat after that."

"And you became lovers?"

There's a stifled sob from Anita. I press on, wanting to exonerate myself.

"I never loved her, if that's what you mean. We had sex, yes. I know it sounds strange, but she was difficult to refuse. She attached herself to me like a stray cat does to anyone who feeds it."

"Had you ever met her previously?"

"No. I'd gone out for a drink at The Riot House nightclub with a mate, Darren Maynard. I gave you his number last night; I expect you'll be speaking to him as well. I think my drink must have been spiked. I woke up in bed the next morning feeling dreadful, and there she was." I avoided eye contact with Anita and kept my gaze on DC Elliott, who checked through his notebook.

"Were you aware that Catherine Taylor was working as a prostitute?"

"No! Absolutely not!" I almost shout it out. "She seemed to have money, but wouldn't tell me where she was getting it from. It didn't occur to me that she might be using my flat as a kno……place to ply her trade."

I feel relieved to get it all out in the open. I'm not sure if I'm mistaken, but suddenly there's a flash of sympathy darting from Anita's eyes to mine. I smile at her and am rewarded with a faint but definite upturn to the corners of her mouth. DC Elliott catches the moment but carries on.

"We spoke to Darren Maynard earlier this morning."

"And?" I'm all ears.

"He confirmed that you passed out in the nightclub that evening, and that he and Catherine Taylor helped you to get home."

I want to cry with relief. I look across the table and see Mike Fairfax and DC Elliott regarding me with something other than hatred. Anita is looking at me the way someone does if you've just given them a million pounds.

"Thank Christ for that! Did he see who spiked my drink?"

"He thought it might have been Catherine Taylor herself."

"That figures." I nod. "If she'd followed me and saw I had a flat in the area where she worked, so to speak, then I was a sitting target if she was homeless."

"Where were you yesterday evening?"

I was waiting for DC Elliott to ask me that one. I look at Anita, who shrugs.

"I was at home with Anita, although I never went into the bedroom. We sat talking on the settee. The first time I saw Cat's body was after I'd walked Anita back to meet her father."

Mike Fairfax visibly relaxes after Anita quickly nods to confirm my statement. Perhaps the knowledge that we didn't go into the bedroom has saved my bacon. Anita looks demurely down at the floor, and I keep my fingers crossed under the table. Something goes *ping* in my brain.

"You may want to check her phone for somebody called Kerry. I think she went to The Riot House with her friend Kerry a couple of nights before she died. Perhaps Kerry can tell you who she met up with there."

I am buoyed up with adrenaline now as I look at DC Elliott and remember one of the last conversations I had with Cat. He nods and makes some notes before asking me one last question.

"The medical officer noted that from the level of decomposition of the body and the amount of rigor mortis, that Miss Taylor would have died somewhere between noon and two o'clock in the afternoon of Friday 7th April. Where were you at this time yesterday?"

"At work. You can check it out with my colleagues."

I am on a roll. The police cannot touch me. DC Elliott puts down his notebook and pen with a faint sigh.

"Yes, we will be doing that. You're free to go, but we'll be contacting you again as part of the investigations into Miss Taylor's death. As she died *in flagrante* so to speak, we'd like you to come back tomorrow and give a DNA sample."

"Sure, but I wasn't there at the time."

"She had just had sexual intercourse. We might be able to match DNA from any semen left inside her body."

"Okay, but it won't be mine."

I stand awkwardly outside the police station with Anita, while

Mike Fairfax stares at us from inside the car and drums his fingers on the steering wheel. I keep a distance between myself and the girl I love, and thank the good Lord that I am off the hook. Anita grins sheepishly.

"Sorry I told you to fuck off."

"Hey, that's okay. I was stupid not to tell you what was going on. I never loved her, but she had nowhere else to go. I sort of took her in, or maybe she took me in." I give a rueful chuckle.

Anita takes a quick glance at her father.

"I've got to go, but I'll text you every day."

"I love you. I've got a holiday booked in July, and I want you to come with me. What d'you say?"

"I'll talk Mum round. She's cool. Perhaps come down and see us one weekend, so that Mum can meet you?"

"Sure. I'll look forward to it."

I wave goodbye as Anita gets in the car, and mouth two words to her as she looks back over her shoulder.

"Love you."

Anita grins and soundlessly forms the words I want to hear.

"Love you too."

CHAPTER 7

I'VE AGREED TO keep in touch with the police while investigations continue, although my instinct is to run as far away as I can. I give a DNA sample, and thankfully there's no match. The holiday Cat had booked in Menorca is still a couple of months away, and I actually feel a pang of regret that somebody like Cat, one of life's unfortunate waifs and strays, will never get to sit her neat little behind on the beach at Arenal d'en Castell. However, so as not to let the holiday go to waste, I decide that somehow or other I'm going to try and take Anita there with me. I sort through a few of Cat's remaining belongings that the police have kindly left *in situ*, find the paperwork, and decide to see if the travel agency can change any details. I know Anita wants to go with me, but I'm going to need some more details from her to give to the travel agent, and so it's a good excuse to phone her. I leave it a day, find her contact number, and then take the biggest chance of my life.

"Hi; it's Paul."

I wait for a tirade of abuse, but none is forthcoming. Instead, my luck is in.

"Hi! I was hoping you'd call!"

Anita sounds on a high. Whatever she's on, I want some.

"Hey! Great to speak to you! So when are you coming down to see me then?"

My luck is in. I'm grinning from ear to ear as I listen to her voice.

"Whenever you're free for the weekend, and your mum doesn't mind me taking over her spare room."

"Oh, she's alright; she's not like Dad at all. You'll be able to sleep in with me."

"Really?" I find I'm shaking my head in disbelief. "Yeah;
I've told her all about you and about Cat. She
realises you didn't have anything to do with Cat's death, and it was just one of those things."

"Absolutely. I'm so glad you see it from my point of view. How about your dad?"

"He came around eventually. He had to when he heard your side of the story. I just wish you'd told me before."

Anita sounds petulant. I can imagine a small but delicious pout playing across her cupid's bow lips. I chuckle.

"And what would you have done if I'd told you Cat was living with me?"

"Er…."

"Yeah; slap my face and run away, I expect."

"Well…."

"Listen; what about the holiday in Menorca I was telling you about? Is your mum okay with it?" I cross two of my fingers as I speak.

"Yeah; she's said it sounds great! How much is it?"

She's excited, and now so am I.

"No money needed; it's all paid
for." "Awesome!"

"I need to go to the travel agents and tell them your name and address though. They'll need your passport details as well, I expect."

"I'll dig out my passport and send you a text in a minute." She sounds like an excited child. "Meanwhile I'll speak to Mum and find out when you can come down."

"I'll wait to hear from you." I sigh with happiness. "Love you."

"Love you too."

Amber Fairfax had kept her married name. I was bowled over by her beauty and poise as she opens the front door to me less than three weeks later. If I hadn't known who she was I might have taken her for Anita's older sister.

"Paul! I'm so glad to meet you! Come in! How was the journey?"

She kisses me on both cheeks as Anita jumps up and down in the background.

"It took about seven hours, and the M6 was a nightmare, but I'm glad I'm here, if only for one night."

Amber laughs as she peruses me. I'm hot, tired, and desperately in need of a drink. She senses this, takes my rucksack, and discreetly disappears into the kitchen to rustle up some fare. Anita squeals, jumps into my arms, and nearly knocks me over.

"Ewww! You're all sweaty!"

"So would you be if you'd just driven four hundred miles!"

It feels great just to kiss her and hold her in my arms. The thought of how close I came to losing her makes me squeeze her even tighter.

"Come on; Mum's got the kettle on. Tea and cake; what d'you say?"

"Is the Pope catholic?"

The kitchen is expensively furnished with teak units, black marble worktops, and indirect lighting. Amber unwraps plates of sandwiches and homemade cakes, and motions for us to sit down.

"Did you get the holiday sorted out, Paul?" I

take a cup of tea gratefully and nod.

"Yes; you're okay about Anita coming with me then?

I try and mask my nervousness in front of who I suppose will be my future mother-in-law. Amber gives me a most charming smile and seats herself next to me.

"Sure, but I think my daughter is old enough to make up her own mind, don't you?"

"Mum, you know I want to go!" Anita bites into a sandwich and grins at me.

I take another sip of tea and carry on getting on the right side of Amber.

"Yes, but it's only polite to ask your mum, seeing as how you're not quite eighteen yet."

"My, my! Such a considerate boy you've got here!" Amber looks at Anita and then back to me. "You'll find I'm a bit more liberal than Mike. In my opinion youngsters will experiment with sex anyway regardless of what their parents' wishes are. You can't hold back nature. Just remember your contraception the pair of you, and you have my blessing."

Wow; I'm temporarily flummoxed. Even worse is the fact that I'm blushing like a fucking thirteen year old still green around the gills. Anita chortles as she chews, enjoying my embarrassment.

"Mum, stop it!"

Amber laughs and ruffles the top of my hair.

"Don't worry Paul; I'll say no more about it, only that don't bother trying to creep into Anita's room tonight. She has a nice big double bed, and she'd like you to share it. Welcome to the family."

My face is as red as an over-ripe tomato. I've never met anyone quite like Amber Fairfax; she's an absolute cracker. How lucky am I to be handed it all on a plate again? An idle thought runs through my head as to whether Amber might be up for a threesome, but at the last minute decide that the man with the golden dick might be pushing his luck a little too far to enquire in that direction.

The second time with Anita in the comfort of her double bed surpasses all my expectations. Although Cat was a pro and up for anything, nothing quite beats the feeling of having no-frills sex with somebody you actually love. As I lie in post-coital bliss with Anita's head on my shoulder, the thought of driving back up the M6 the following day fills me with rampant dismay.

CHAPTER 8

I FIND MYSELF working all the overtime possible during the week, and spending the proceeds on petrol driving up and down the M6 at weekends, which works out cheaper than taking the train. At work people complain that I've turned into one of those loved-up observers of life through rose-tinted specs, but I can't help it; I'm deeply in love with a girl who seems to think I'm the next best thing to anti-wrinkle cream. And that's not all; my future mother-in-law and I seem to be getting on like a house on fire. At the end of the working day I find that I don't want to go home to my lonely flat, and seem to spend an inordinate amount of time either talking on the phone to Anita, or drinking in the Rat & Pigeon with Darren, who is of the opinion that I'm turning into some kind of boring arsehole.

On a Thursday towards the end of June the police contact me. They've gone over the CCTV footage from the camera situated opposite The Riot House nightclub. They want me to go to the station to see if I can identify a middle-aged man who leaves with Cat on the night of the 5th April, less than 48 hours before her death. With some degree of trepidation I turn up at the station after work and sit through the grainy shots (why is CCTV footage always blurry?) but to me the bloke just looks like he might be one of her punters. They walk away together down the street, and I shake my head none the wiser. DC Elliott lets me know the footage will be shown on Saturday's Crimewatch programme, and that Cat's friend and cohort Kerry Tricker (an apt name for a hooker if ever there was one) will be dressing up as Cat for the TV viewers and exiting the nightclub with one of the detectives who apparently slightly resembles the saddo on the CCTV film.

I still wonder if the police think I'm the culprit, but all my alibis and DNA check out and I know they've got nothing on me. DC Elliott even nods when I ask him if I can go on holiday to Menorca; I can't believe my luck. I pick up the phone and call Anita as soon as I step out into the street.

"Hi; guess what?"

"What?"

She sounds upbeat as usual. "Menorca is definitely on." "Cool! I've bought a new bikini." "Mmm….you'll look better without it though." "Cheeky!"

I can't wait for the following night to be able to see her again. We talk about absolutely nothing for the next half an hour.

A forty-something builder type opens the door and looks me up and down when I arrive at Amber's place late on the Friday night. I haven't seen him before, but Anita runs down the stairs and grins at me.

"Hi Paul! This is Dave, Mum's friend."

"Hello."

I hold out my right arm towards him. My hand is enveloped in a firm, muscular grip.

"Alright?"

Dave seems to be a man of few words. We size each other up, and I reckon I can take him on if push comes to shove.

"I'm fine thanks."

I take an instant dislike to the bloke straight away. When Amber comes out and gives me a hug, I feel his gaze boring into me like a creeping death.

"I've left a cold supper out for you. You must be famished."

I grin at Amber and turn my back on Dave.

"You're not far wrong. Thanks. I'll have something to eat and a shower if you don't mind."

"Not at all. Help yourself. I'm going up to bed now, so I'll see you in the morning."

I look quizzically at Anita as Dave follows Amber up the stairs. Anita shrugs.

"He's alright. He and Mum have been going out for ages."

"I haven't seen him before. He's sleeping here tonight then?"

"Of course." Anita chuckles. "You never hear them at it though, so don't worry."

"What does he do? Is he a hod carrier?" I look up the stairs with disdain.

"I think he's a bouncer. She likes a bit of rough."

"He's that alright."

It's so good to feel Anita's naked body on top of mine. My hands fondle her breasts and she throws her head back in a climax as she rides me. I gasp when I ejaculate too quickly, forgetting about Amber and Dave in the next room.

"Shh!" Anita grins and flops forward onto my chest. "Shut up!"

"They're probably doing it as well!" I caress her hair and whisper into her ear. "I can't wait for our holiday. We can make as much noise as we like."

She giggles and then snuggles up to me. I feel like I'm in the closest thing to heaven that there can be down here on earth.

Although I don't want to be reminded of Cat's death, the temptation to turn on the TV the following evening in time for Crimewatch is overwhelming. Amber and Dave go out for dinner, and so there's just Anita and I left in the sitting room. We cuddle together on the settee and I fiddle with the TV remote control.

"Turn it on if you want." Anita wriggles onto my lap and sighs.

"Okay; they're running through Cat's last hours on Crimewatch tonight."

"Ewwww! I don't want to watch *that*!" Anita shakes her head.

"I need to see it." I press the 'on' switch'. "I might recognise the face this time if I see it on screen."

"You said you didn't know who it was when the police showed him to you."

Anita sounds petulant, but I stand my ground.

"Yeah, I know; but just humour me.   I'll turn it off as

soon as it's over and we can go out somewhere if you like."

"Oh…*okay*…if I must."

She jumps off my lap and curls up silently next to me. Ignoring her sulks I stare transfixed at the screen while the intro plays. Fortunately the police reconstruction of Cat's last couple of days is first on. I only saw Kerry once, but now wearing a blonde wig and dressed in the clothes Cat wore on the night, she looks remarkably like the girl who sought me out and whom I should have loved but never did. Kerry exits The Riot House on the arm of a burly middle-aged man wearing jeans and a bomber jacket, and they walk along the road and disappear around a corner. Anita fidgets in her seat.

"Is that it? Can we turn it off now?"

"Just wait and see if there's anything else first."

A close up of the man's face I had already seen at the police station fills the screen. I am still none the wiser. However, by the end of the programme the announcer seems quite animated and informs viewers that the switchboard is alive with people calling in who apparently recognise the man's features. As I switch off the TV and take Anita in my arms it occurs to me that DC Elliott will have his work cut out interviewing them all.

It's not until I'm packing for Menorca a few weeks later that my phone buzzes with an incoming call from the police. I laugh ruefully as I wonder how many people have their own pet detective constable on hand as a phone contact.

"Mr McAdam?"

"That's me."

I start to wonder what he wants. I look at my packed suitcase, and hope to God I don't have to cancel the holiday.

"Did you see the Crimewatch programme?"

"Yes. Did you get much feedback?"

"Sure did. I'm just ringing to let you know that somebody recognised her husband coming out of The Riot House with Catherine Taylor."

"Oh?" I am all ears.

"Yeah; we picked him up for questioning, but he denied the murder."

"As the saying goes, he would, wouldn't he?" I chuckle.

"His DNA didn't match the semen sample." "So you're no further forward then?"

"Not yet, but we'll get there in the end. When are you off to Menorca?"

"Tomorrow. I'm staying near Stansted and meeting Anita there tonight."

As I end the call with false pleasantries I can't help but wonder why the fucker is still keeping tabs on me.

CHAPTER 9

AS I WAIT for Anita in the foyer of the Radisson Hotel at Stansted airport I start to get excited at hearing the planes flying overhead every two minutes or so. To think that we'll be alone together in Menorca for a whole fortnight is enough to put a permanent grin on my face. In fact I'm still smiling when I see Amber's car appearing outside complete with 'L' plates, and Anita sitting grim-faced and tense in the driver's seat. Amber leaps out and plants a kiss on my cheek.

"She's terrified, but she did it!"

I give Amber a hug and race around to where Anita, sweating and sighing with relief, is climbing out from behind the steering wheel.

"Now I've driven here through the London traffic I can drive anywhere!"

I envelop her in a bear hug. Her back is wet with the stress of ensuring they arrived with all four limbs still intact.

"You'll soon be driving up to me in Scotland!"

"We'll see about that after my test. Now I just want to have a bath and relax."

Amber lifts Anita's suitcase out of the boot, and then goes around to the driver's seat after giving her daughter a final hug.

"Look after my little girl, Paul. She's all I've got."

"No worries, Amber. We'll call you from Stansted in a fortnight when we land again. I'll bring her home to you."

Grinning at each other like two Cheshire cats and with our arms around each other, I trundle Anita's suitcase to the reception desk with my free hand and she checks in. Then finding we are alone in the lift we kiss passionately, both of us now highly aroused at the thought of the evening to come and the chance to spend the next two weeks in each other's company. Locked away in our hotel room I can't even wait for Anita to get out of the bath. Stripping off as I see her sitting there soaping herself, I jump in on top of her, causing her to roar with laughter and water to cascade over the top of the bath onto the floor.

"Paul! Stop it!"

She giggles and tries to push me away half-heartedly, but I'm all for learning if sex in the bath is pleasant. I find out to my delight that it definitely is.

Thank Christ Anita's used to flying back and forth to Edinburgh. I've never been on a plane in my entire miserable life, and quickly learn that airports involve a lot of queueing and waiting about. As soon as we line up to check our bags in then it's time to join the depressingly long queue of people snaking along cordoned-off waiting areas to go through security, and then blow me down with a feather I have to queue again to buy a newspaper and a bottle of water at £2.50 a go for the 2 hour flight. As I join another queue to go through the last barrier and actually get onto the fucking plane itself, Anita looks at me and grins.

"Cheer up. There'll be a nice long queue at Customs and then Baggage Collection at the other end."

"Marvellous."

I can't be irritable for too long, as I'm with the best girl that ever lived. However, as soon as I try and fold my long legs into the cramped space between the seats while a screaming toddler across the aisle from us gives it all he's got, my resurged bonhomie takes a sudden downturn.

"Have I got to sit like this for 2 hours?"

Anita laughs and switches on her Kindle.

"Yep. Read your paper and zone out. It'll all be over soon."

The toddler's fury knows no bounds. Its face is blood red as its mother tries to wrestle it into a seat belt on her lap. The cabin crew are giving instructions of how to jump out of the plane if it goes into a nosedive. I'm trying to listen but all I can hear is the toddler screaming. I have a sudden mental image of bashing its head on the floor and shutting it up for good, but in all reality I know its mother probably wouldn't go for that option.

I give a rueful laugh; even the bloody pilot has to queue on the runway. As the engines roar for take-off, the toddler's whine is temporarily drowned out as the plane picks up speed. I like the thrill of speeding, and look out of the window as the ground rushes away. Anita doesn't even look up from her Kindle, so bored is she with the whole thing. I can't help the next remark that comes out of my mouth.

"It's exciting, isn't it?"

"I don't think so. Don't you get out much, Paul?" She yawns and sighs.

I decide to omit the fact that I've only been on a National Express coach to London a few times. My ears pop and burn as the plane climbs higher, but then surprisingly it levels out and doesn't feel as though we're moving at all. We're above the clouds, and it's a glorious sunny day. The toddler shuts up and falls asleep, its mother relaxes and closes her eyes, and suddenly I'm near to God's heaven and all's right with the world.

Mahon airport is cool and spacious, so I'm not ready for the wall of heat that hits me as we step out of the main doors and follow the rep's instructions towards minibus number 84. Anita runs along nimbly with her Kindle in one hand and her handbag in the other, while I trundle behind lugging both suitcases and sweating like I've just run two marathons back to back.

"Come on! I can see the bus!"

"What have you got in this case...... bricks?"

"It's my chastity belt." Anita laughs as she steps onto the minibus.

"Aren't you supposed to be wearing
it?" "I forgot."

"Looks like I'm in luck then."

I grin at her and heave her suitcase into the back of the minibus with mine, and then sink gratefully into the seat beside her and turn up the cold air flow above my head.

"It's never this hot in Edinburgh."

"Make the most of it. It'll be raining when you get home."

Another four couples climb onto the bus with the rep bringing up the rear. The driver introduces himself as Rafa, and then we set off. I snuggle with Anita for a while and gaze idly out of the window half-listening as the rep points out stunted olive trees, odd whitewashed houses dotted about reflecting the sun, dry stone walls covered in bramble, and fig trees and tamarisks as we approach the coast on the ME9 motorway. I'm not that bothered about looking at dry stone walls, and prefer cuddling my bird. After about 30 minutes the driver stops to drop off three couples at a hotel near a splash park. It looks good, and I wonder if our own hotel is going to be as good as the one I can see before me.

CHAPTER 10

SO COMFORTABLE AM I with Anita's head on my shoulder that I'm nearly dozing off when the minibus slows down and comes to a halt on a steep hill outside our hotel. Reluctantly I shake Anita awake, who leaps up excitedly like a scalded cat.

"We're here! Come on!"

Another rep's handing out glasses of fruit juice and hot flannels in the foyer, as we drag our cases in through the hotel's revolving glass doors. I suffer a brief pang of guilt that Cat should be wiping her face with the flannel instead of Anita, but then after the checking-in process I find I'm all fired up and ready to enjoy my holiday. We pick up keys to a room on the 6th floor, squeeze ourselves and our bags into the lift with a hugely overweight couple, and breathe a sigh of relief when it stops with a judder at the sixth floor.

"Thank God it didn't get stuck!" Anita whispers conspiratorially as the lift doors close again behind us.

"I'm taking the stairs every time now." I grin. "Whichever one of us finds the room first gets to rip the other one's clothes off."

"You're on!"

I'm lumbered down with two heavy cases, so Anita wins

the bet. To my eternal delight I'm stark bollock naked within seconds of the room door closing, and Anita's not far behind.

It's only when we get out of bed that we discover the spectacular view over Arenal d'en Castell's horseshoe bay from our 6th floor vantage point. With the sheet wrapped around us and our noses pressed up against the window, we take in pretty whitewashed villas with swimming pools, the clear blue waters of the bay, a white sandy beach, and three neat rows of straw sunshades on the sand with sunbeds underneath.

"It's paradise!" Anita turns away, rummages around in her case, and brings out a bikini and sarong. "Come on, let's go down to the beach."

I'm used to hills in Scotland, and it's just as well we've got young legs as there's 144 steps down from the road to the beach. Anita counts them as we descend.

"We've got a long climb back up to the hotel."

She grumbles good-naturedly and I give her hand a squeeze.

"I'll carry you back up."

"You'll be good for nothing for the rest of the day; I weigh nearly nine stones!"

"Oh, you'll find I can rise to any

occasion." "Trust you to think about *that*!"

"I'm a bloke, aren't I?"

The sea is calm and inviting. Other couples sprawl out on sunbeds or sit bolt upright doing lighthouse impressions with their gaze on young children. I plan to join the former, and grab two empty beds. Anita brings out some factor 50, and we lie there resembling two roasting chickens under the hot afternoon sun.

"Fifteen Euros please."

I'm brought out of my reverie by the sunbed attendant appearing out of nowhere and rubbing his hands with glee at the sight of two pasty British tourists with money in their pockets. I'm just about to try and haggle him down a bit, when Anita produces two notes from her purse.

"There you go."

"Gracias Senorita."

I watch him leer down Anita's cleavage and suddenly want to give him the Scottish kiss.

"Why didn't you haggle?" I stare at his back as he walks away.

"It's not the done thing; you just pay up and shut up."

"Sod that; I'll beat him down tomorrow." "Good luck with that then."

Anita settles back on the sunbed. Out of the corner of my eye I can see a bronzed, topless Spanish woman throwing a Frisbee to her boyfriend down by the shoreline. The sight is utterly mesmerising, nicely augmented as other equally half-naked females stroll past me quite unconcerned.

"Stop being such a lech!"

Anita's following my gaze, and I'm well and truly nicked. Adding to this is a growing erection at the sight of a bountiful pair of jugs that would win first prize in a Miss Titty 2000 contest. This is definitely *not* Porty Beach. I turn over on my stomach and reluctantly close my eyes.

"I don't know what you're talking about."

Appeased, Anita relaxes again and I watch the rhythmic rise and fall of her chest, amongst other locations south of the border. My girl has a beautiful body, which I plan to invade as often as I'm allowed to during the next fortnight.

Just before dinner we join a group of newbies, and ovine-like file into the upstairs bar to meet the rep who we've already met on the minibus. I start to make sheep noises, but Anita digs me in the ribs.

"Shhhh! We get to book excursions at this meeting."

"How much is it going to cost me?" I look with suspicion at the rep.

"Nothing. Mum's given us money for trips."

"Wow; good old Amber." I nod in approval.

We settle for a ride in a 24ft power boat along the north coast with a chance of swimming and snorkelling, a trip to the caves of Xoroi and the market at Mahon, and a visit to Cala Galdana beach and Binibeca, the 'sugar cube' village which Anita has already Googled before we arrived and wants to see. I can't believe my luck; first the holiday was paid for by Cat, and now the excursions by my as yet unaware future mother-in-law. I am without doubt one seriously lucky bastard.

The evening entertainment isn't up to much, and so we return to our room and make our own. Anita's moans during an obviously deeply satisfying session of oral sex I reckon must echo all the way down the corridor towards the lift shaft. She's fired me up into a frenzy, and I hope to God the other punters are downstairs watching the duo doing a bad imitation of Richard and Karen Carpenter, otherwise we'll never be able to face our neighbours at the breakfast buffet in the morning.

CHAPTER 11

I WATCH ANITA as the wind whips through her hair. She reaches up, ties it back, and smiles at me as the power boat picks up speed out of the port of Addaia on the second day of our holiday. I'm aware that the male halves of the other three middle aged couples on the boat are slavering as Anita removes her sarong and t-shirt, and sunbathes in a gold coloured string bikini.

"This is awesome!"

I wasn't quite sure if she would like the choppy waters, but I'm relieved that she seems to be enjoying herself.

"How about some snorkelling when it stops in a while?" "I'm not putting one of those mouthpieces anywhere near my mouth." She looks with disdain at a pile of snorkels. "Who knows where they've been?"

"The salt water will kill the germs anyway." I grin. "I'm going in."

"Fill your boots. I'll sit and watch."

I wish she would cover up a bit. Even the boat's captain seems distracted. Also the three forty-something women keeping a discreet eye on their men definitely do not appear to be enjoying themselves. I can tell that Anita is lapping up the attention; flaunting the handiwork of the divine potter with which she has been so bounteously endowed.

"Put your top back on." I hiss into her ear over the thrum of the engine. "Everyone's staring at you."

Reluctantly, but to my relief, she dons a t-shirt. The captain points out various points of interest along the coastline, and tells us about Sir Richard Kane, born in County Antrim and appointed Governor of Menorca in 1733, who reformed the Menorcan legal system, built roads, and improved trade. I listen with half an ear but can't take my eyes off my girl. Long-dead governors aren't doing it for me, but Anita is. She grins with the knowledge that I'm ablaze with lust.

After about an hour we drop anchor in a shallow cove. Only one other small boat is anchored there, and the beach is empty except for a couple sunbathing stark naked, who hurriedly jump up, plunge into the sea, and swim back towards their boat when they see us approaching.

The blue water of the Mediterranean sparkles invitingly, and I'm baking hot. Two of the other women step gingerly down the boat's ladder, and all the men jump off the side, including myself. Anita takes photos of us from the safety of her white leather seat.

"Come on in!" I wave to her. "It's lovely and warm!" To my surprise she stands up, moves over to the ladder, and eases herself down into the water, still wearing her t-shirt.

"The woman sitting opposite was staring daggers at me, so I thought I'd join you."

We leave the other men behind snorkelling and swim over to explore what looks like an opening to a cave. Inside it's cool out of the sun; the water laps around our waists, and I'm as horny as a sack full of rabbits. I pull Anita towards me out of sight of the others.

"I can't keep my hands off you; you're doing my head in."

She laughs, and the sound echoes around the cave. We kiss passionately and under the water I slowly let my hand wander down into the fleecy depths inside the front of Anita's bikini bottom.

"Stop it! Someone's swimming over, I can hear them!"

She pulls away and floats out to the entrance of the cave, just as one of the men swims up to us. I dive under the sea away from him and try to quell a growing erection. As I grab hold of one of her legs and slide my hand ever upwards under the water, she offers no resistance and wraps her legs around mine.

"Ever had sex in the sea?"

She's teasing me, knowing it's going to be impossible to accomplish without being detected. However, as I turn around I can see the man swimming away again. I call her bluff and indicate in the direction of the cave.

"No, but there's always a first time."

The captain is chilling out on deck, the one middle-aged woman left on board is dozing, and all the other swimmers are now some distance away. Giggling with a sudden excitement, we swim back to the cave. She removes her bikini bottom effortlessly and guides my swollen member in whilst I hold her legs around me and use the weight of my body to press her against the wall of the cave. I come almost at once; the relief is overwhelming. Eager to please, I then let her rub herself against me, which she does with a delightfully increasing urgency.

"Don't make a sound." I whisper in her ear as I thrust away. "We don't need any explorers coming in."

I can feel her shuddering orgasm as surprisingly, she adheres to my wishes. We stand glued together until we hear the boat's engine starting up.

"Shit! I must have dropped by bikini bottom in the water!"

Panic-stricken, Anita searches around for the elusive piece of string that just about covers her dignity. With all lewd thoughts rapidly departing, I pull up my trunks and dive under the water, opening my eyes against the salt. The cave is dark and I can't see the bloody thing anywhere. I surface with nothing in my hands, and see all hope fade from her eyes.

"Pull your t-shirt down and go last up the ladder. Did you bring any shorts in the rucksack?"

"No, but I've still got the sarong thank God."

She looks close to tears, and I try with some success to stifle a grin.

"You'll have to wear that, or have your fanny on show for the rest of the trip."

"Go back quickly then, and chuck it down to me in the water!"

Oh, the perils of having sex in the sea. At least I can chalk that one up to experience. Now we'll have to work on joining the Mile High Club on the way home.

The minibus picking us up at the port has thick towels on the seats, which is just as well considering we're all soaking wet. While we wait for one of the other couples to get in I give Anita a wink as she shuffles up next to me in the back, wearing her gold sarong.

·"Alright?"

"I'm never going swimming with you again." She whispers. "That bikini cost me thirty five quid."

"Take me shopping along Oxford Street when we get home, and I'll buy you a crotchless one."

"Great. You'll have to teach me how to swim with my legs crossed then."

Thank goodness the driver appears to speak little English. We're still giggling ten minutes later when the bus pulls up back at the hotel.

CHAPTER 12

MY LONG FACE shows a healthy distaste of organised coach trips, as we join a line of twittering middle-agers on the first Tuesday who, like Anita, are intent on seeing Binibeca Vell. I notice that we're the youngest ones on the coach. I get a dig in the ribs and a frosty look when I mention I'd rather go down to the beach, but Anita wants to see the 'sugar cube' tourist spot even though I found out on Google that surprise, surprise, it was built in 1972 to resemble an old fishing village and isn't authentic at all.

The tour guide for the day begins to drone on as soon as the coach starts off. The day is partly saved when I find out there'll be a 2 hour stop on Binibeca Nou beach in the afternoon. I cheer up, give Anita a kiss, and settle down to whatever the day will bring.

First off is a stop at Mahon market. The sun is a blistering furnace as we all step off the coach in Esplanada Square. I have an urge to make more sheep noises as we follow the middle-agers towards the stalls, but think better of it. I'm sure the stall holders are mentally rubbing their hands with glee at the sight of another load of pasty faced tourists, and I take my wallet out of my back pocket to keep a closer eye on it. Anita's like a kid in a sweet shop as she darts from one stall to another, but to me it seems like they're all selling the same tat. I don't want to buy anything. However, it seems as though I'm handy for carrying Anita's many purchases.

When we set off for Binibeca Vell I can see another 5 coaches have pulled up in Esplanada Square. With a rueful grin I mention to Anita how convenient it is for the locals that these trips are always planned for Tuesdays.

Twenty minutes' drive from Mahon is Binibeca Vell, on the south coast. I kneel up and look out the back window of the coach as it parks. I see four recycling bins and a bottle bank. Anita follows my gaze.

"This is sure picturesque." I sigh.

"Wait until we get out; I'm sure you'll love it."

I'm suddenly carried along with Anita's enthusiasm as we leave the middle-agers behind and walk past the old harbour. The blinding sun shining down on the narrow alleyways between the whitewashed villas with their painted lime rooves creates a chiaroscuro of light and shade, and we take heed of the frequent notices for silence along the tiny cobbled alleys. I know it's a fake village and probably only inhabited by holidaymakers, but nevertheless it has a great olde-worlde charm to it. We wander about, lost in the feel of the past that Antonio Sintes decided quite cleverly in 1972 that we needed to experience.

An hour passes by in an instant and ravenous and thirsty, we decide to stop by a small complex filled with bars and restaurants. I'm chilled and in love. I've forgotten all about Cat, and only have eyes for Anita as we sit down on red canvas chairs under a sunshade at one of the outside tables.

It's still too early for the Spanish to think about lunch, and we seem to be the only customers in the place. Anita looks good enough to eat as she orders tapas, salad, and a glass of Coto Mayor. I'm amazed at her *savoir faire*, nod blindly at the waiter to say I'll have some of the same, and then turn my gaze back.

"You're right. There's something about this place." I look around appreciatively.

"Told you." Anita gives a trilling laugh. "And you with a long face on all morning."

The service is on the slow side, but I don't care. As I sip my glass of wine I'm suffused with a warmth and general bonhomie which has nothing to do with the outside temperature or the alcohol. I reach across the table with one hand and grab Anita's fingers with my own.

"I love you." I sigh.

She grins at me and gives my hand a squeeze.

"What's brought that on?"

"I don't know." I shake my head. "But there's more."

"More?"

"Yeah, more."

"What more?"

She's laughing now as I stand up, walk around to her side of the table, drop down to my knees, and take both of her hands in mine.

"We've only known each other for a short while, but you're the girl I want to spend the rest of my life with. Anita, will you marry me?"

I don't know what's come over me; it must be the ambience of the place. Darren would be crapping himself with laughter now if he saw me. I look at my love beseechingly as a slight breeze ruffles the red checked tablecloths and a stray cat slinks by languidly in the heat. There's a terrible moment of silence before one word slips out of Anita's surprised mouth.

"Yes."

I hook both arms around her waist and press my head to her chest in relief. I'm still in the same kneeling position when the waiter brings out the tapas. I rise to my feet and explain to him as best I can that I've just proposed to my girlfriend. He gives me a high five and lets us have the meal for free.

We lie facing each other in part shade on Binibeca Nou beach. The sand is blistering on my feet, which protrude over the end of the hotel's towel that is definitely only allowed to be used around their own swimming pool. Well, as far as I'm concerned, rules are for breaking aren't they?

Anita runs a finger up and down my arm.

"Can we get married at Gretna Green?"

I sit up, look at her, and think about it.

"Why? Won't your parents approve? Have we got to elope then?"

"No, silly. Mum loves you and I'm sure Dad will go along with it. It's just that it'll be a bit different, won't it?"

"I suppose so." I nod. "Let's look into it when we get back."

"I love you Paul." Anita sighs and closes her eyes.

"I love you too. Sorry I can't produce an engagement ring. Asking you to marry me was a spur of the moment thing. I'll buy you one when we get home."

"Lovely."

The waves crashing against the shore are soporific, and I

lay back down. Full of tapas and wine I'm close to nodding off, but I have to make sure we're back on the coach in an hour's time. Anita's steady breathing tells me she's already asleep, and I feast my eyes on her unlined skin and blonde eyelashes. I can hardly believe my luck that this girl will soon be my bride. I'm the most fortunate bastard who ever lived.

The next day we get adventurous, take some advice from the hotel rep, and catch one of the local buses into Mahon. Anita has changed her mind and decides that she wants an engagement ring right away to present to her mother on returning home. I've no idea how Amber will take the news, let alone Mike Fairfax, but we're excited about our future and now I'm eager to buy my girl a token of my love.

There's a wealth of little shops surrounding the beachfront area at Mahon. I've got all fingers and toes crossed that Anita won't pick out something too expensive. I'm not as stupid with money as Darren is, but then again I wasn't born with a silver spoon stuck up my arse either. We ask about and are directed down a little alleyway to where local craftsmen are working silver and gold into jewellery for the tourists. Examples of necklaces, rings and earrings are in the shop window, and I can see that the prices are not out of my reach. It's the perfect place for us, and Anita's through the door as soon as I give the nod.

I follow her towards several blue velvet trays containing finished rings, which are protected under a glass case and are being presided over by an unctuous male shop assistant. After some deliberation she points to a band consisting of many small, silver hearts joined together all the way around the ring. The shop assistant tells us in broken English that it's one of a kind. I like its design, and I can tell by Anita's squeals that she's already fallen in love with it. I do a quick calculation in my head at the sight of the 16,600 peseta price tag, and come up with a figure close to 70 pounds. She tries it on, and it's a perfect fit.

Back in the privacy of our room after we had changed for dinner, I take the ring out of its box and place it on the third finger of Anita's left hand. She throws her arms around my neck and I hold her tight. I want us to stay like this forever.

When I check my phone just before I get into bed, I'm irritated at the sight of a message from DC Elliott.

'Hi. Hope you're having a good holiday. Just to let you know that Catherine Taylor's parents have put up a £20,000 reward for information leading to the arrest of their daughter's murderer. We should start getting some information hopefully soon.'

I stare at the words for a moment or two, digesting the information. This is the first time that I've heard about Cat's parents. I'd foolishly taken it for granted she had grown up in care and had nobody. The parents are obviously quite a well-off couple, and I realise that the message throws a completely new slant on proceedings. Soon every Tom, Dick and Harry in Edinburgh will be coming up with all kinds of stories and falling over each other to get at the money.

"Come to bed, baby." Anita purrs and stretches out naked.

I join her, but for once I can't think about anything other than how that sanctimonious fucker's message from a thousand miles away has ruined the rest of my evening. I want to smash the bastard's head in.

I hope it takes him forever to follow up all the leads.

CHAPTER 13

AFTER BREAKFAST THERE'S time left before the next coach trip to check out Gretna Green on the hotel's computer in the foyer. Anita, fingers of her left hand splayed out on the table to show any passing guests her new engagement ring, is already champing at the bit to get the wedding arranged, and so we sit there like two excited chimpanzees at a tea party. Anita points to information underneath the famous blacksmith's shop.

"Look; it says we can phone up and book a date! We just have to both be over sixteen, have our birth certificates handy, fill out their marriage notice forms, pay the fee, and then find two witnesses."

DC Elliott's message is still fresh in my mind. I decide to waste no more time.

"Let's do it! Just us two though; I don't want all the relatives. What d'you say?" I kiss her cheek and eagerly wait for her reply.

"Perfect!" Anita's virtually jumping for joy. "Even better, we won't tell anyone until we've done it!"

"Yeah!" I'm riding along on a wave of euphoria now. "We'll pull two witnesses in off the street; no worries."

"I'll make a note of the phone number." Anita takes a pen and notebook out of her bag. "We'll phone them from our room this afternoon when we get back from the trip."

"Baa, baa, baa." I make some loud sheep noises. "Baa, baa."

At least there's some younger couples this time on the coach, and the atmosphere's livelier. I don't know why middle-agers just sit in silence on these trips. They don't even seem to talk to their partners much, and the rep has to repeat everything twice to get some sort of reaction from them; it's peculiar. Perhaps by the time you get to fifty there's nothing much left to say?

We're going to be dropped off at Cala Galdana beach for a few hours. Anita spends most of the journey talking nineteen to the dozen and flashing her engagement ring at a few younger couples, who to my acute embarrassment start singing that Cliff Richard song you always hear in those Frankie and Benny restaurants. I try and take it all in good part, but I just want to get off the coach and have my girl all to myself.

A crowd of twenty-somethings pull us along with them over the bridge towards the beach, leaving the middle-agers behind to take six hours getting off the coach. I don't even know their names, but Anita's made friends with all of them. To my chagrin it seems that we're now in with the in-crowd. I sigh and hang back, putting my arm around Anita's waist.

"Let's ditch this lot in a minute and find a cave somewhere."

Anita laughs and punches me playfully on the shoulder.

"Oh, God; not again! Come on, don't be a grouch!

Tony's been here before; he knows the best spot to sunbathe."

"Oh he does, does he?" I look with disdain at a cropped ginger head out in front. "I'm not sitting on a sunbed next to that wanker."

However, because Anita has such a sunny nature, I can't stay angry for long. I resign myself to a few hours of having to share my girl with what eventually turns out to be a pleasant group of three other young couples. We swap life stories as we eat takeaway burgers and chips whilst sitting under a tree on the beach, which seems a grade up from our own resort. The whole area is flat, it's more geared towards families, and there seems much more to do. As we chat I purposefully omit the Cat fiasco, and find that another guy, Malcolm, also hails from Edinburgh although currently lives in Newcastle. His girl Tina takes a shine to Anita, and the two of them even swap phone numbers. Before you can say Jack Robinson Tina and Malcolm have agreed to be our witnesses.

We're in the hub of the resort next to a couple of bars, a café, a first aid post, toilets, and a lifeguard station. Music blasts out from one of the bars, and I begin to relax. Tony buys the first round of beers, Malcolm the second, Steve the third, and I feel obliged to keep my end up. I walk over and order four pints of lager, two gin and tonics, and two cocktails. As I sink another glass I lay down on my sunbed, full of good cheer and the mellowing effects of four pints of Estrella Damm. Anita leans over and gives me a kiss on the nose.

"Love you. Who sent you that message last night?"
I think back in my foggy brain to the previous evening.
"That cop Elliott." I yawn. "Love you too."

Anita strokes the hair on my chest.

"What did he want?"

"He said there's a twenty thousand pound reward for finding Cat's killer." The last few words come out only slightly slurred.

"Really?" She sits up.

"Yeah." I close my eyes. "Every Jock in Edinburgh will be phoning in. It'll take the bastard months to follow the leads up."

"Why did he text you on holiday?" "'Cos he's a wanker."

When I wake up I look at my watch and grimace. It's three o'clock and we should have caught the coach an hour ago to travel over to see the San Martorellet dancing horses. The other three couples are still asleep, including Anita. I shake myself awake and shrug. *Aye, what the hell. We might as well stay here now and catch a taxi back later on.*

I yawn and try to clear my head. Tony and Malcolm are stirring. As Tony checks the time on his phone he lets out an expletive.

"Fuck!"

His one word wakes all the others. We all look at each other and burst out laughing. Anita, ever one to have looked up the trips beforehand on Google, comes to our rescue.

"It's only a couple of miles from here to San Martorellet. Let's phone for some taxis. Hopefully we'll still be able to catch some of the show."

Hastily we gather our possessions and march back quickly over the bridge. I have a slight headache. The Cala Galdana hotel sits grand and luxuriously in front of us, and the receptionist is very obliging. She gabbles away in Spanish, and five minutes later we're all piling into two taxis. Thankfully the fare is pennies, as the horse show is not too far away. We ignore frosty stares from the rep and all the middle-agers, and slink into our seats to catch the rest of the show. Even better than watching the poor creatures made to rear up countless times for the delectation of the audience is the free ride back to the hotel on the coach and the chance to doze off again. Darren's always telling me I can't hold my beer.

As we're an hour in front of the UK, the Gretna office is still open when we return to our room and pick up the phone. There's a vacancy in the Blacksmith's Shop for Saturday September 2nd at 11.30 with a photographer included, and a hotel room is available that night at the Smiths and for the previous day. I give out our names and addresses, and as I replace the receiver we jump up and down at the thought of our marriage forms there waiting for us to fill in and send off when we return home from holiday. There are another few pay-days in-between now and September 2nd, and I'm certain I can manage the fee. Anita says her mother never opens any post that's not addressed to her. We can get away with it.

We come down to earth and discuss where we're going to live. Anita wants to stay with me in Edinburgh, and says she'll make enquiries regarding transferring her college course to a similar one that will be more local to us, and will look for weekend work to help with the bills. For the actual wedding itself she decides to be brave and to ask her mother for a loan of the car the day before in order, so she will say, to drive up and see her father for a weekend visit to surprise him. I can see one problem with this, and tell her so.

"Anita, you haven't passed your driving test yet, and it's a 7 hour drive."

Unperturbed, she shrugs her shoulders.

"I've got my test booked for my birthday on 9th August. It'll be a piece of cake. "Just wear a short skirt."

"Don't be a sexist pig. Anyway, we're not supposed to be together on the day before our wedding. It's unlucky. I hope you've booked me a separate room in the hotel."

"You must be joking!" I stare at her in amazement.

She laughs, and I'm not sure if she was serious or not. She shrugs her shoulders and looks at me.

"Okay then, well, by the time I've driven up most of the day will be gone anyway."

"We're lucky; don't worry." I kiss her. "Nothing will ever go wrong with our marriage."

CHAPTER 14

A WEE SPANISH boy and girl happily building sandcastles with their parents suddenly takes me back to the misery of my childhood; the terrible holidays on Porty Beach when all that would ever happen would be Mum nagging because Dad was drunk again, and Dad shouting about how he was only drinking to drown out the sound of Mum's nagging. Terry would be causing mayhem to try and gain their attention. Dad would take out his anger and frustration on Terry and me, causing Terry to play up even more and me to withdraw more and more into myself, until at last, the day of judgement came as a surprise to all of us.

As I gaze at the happy family picture in front of me, Anita's voice brings me out of my reverie.

"Penny for them?"

"Eh?" I sigh.

"You're miles away."

"All I ever wished for was *that*." I indicate towards the Spanish family with a flick of my thumb. "Instead it was World War Three whenever they were together. Thank God it's in the past. As I kid though, I could never get what I wanted, which was for us all to be like that bloody Walton family on TV."

"But now you can." Anita turned over on her sunbed.

"Too right." I nod in agreement. "As soon as I saw you I knew what I wanted, and that I'd move heaven and earth to make it happen."

Anita chuckles and closes her eyes.

"Yeah; I bet you only wanted to get into my knickers."

"No, not necessarily." I lie. "I was prepared to wait for that. With you I saw the kind of life that was the complete opposite to how I'd been brought up. I knew we could make it happen, you and I. Our children will never hear a cross word between us."

I lie on my back on the sunbed and hold out my arm towards Anita. A warm hand finds its way to mine.

"Our *children?* Steady on, I'm barely out of nappies myself!"

"Whenever you want them." I hastily add. "I'll be only too happy to do my bit."

"Yeah, I bet you will." Anita chuckles again. "You're happy to do your bit even if I *don't* want to get pregnant."

"Well, I can't deny it." I smile. "Making babies is a very pleasant occupation."

When we wake up the Spanish family have gone, although the happy family dream I've kept hidden until now but have always been so desperate to create is still within my grasp. I look at my girl slapping on the Factor 50, and give her silent kudos at emerging from a broken home without the anxiety, anger, and fear of powerlessness which have plagued me all my adult life. Ian and Molly McAdam had a marriage made in hell, and I'm sure it would have been better if they had divorced when Terry and I were young kids. Their legacy lives on in Paul Christopher McAdam, a fucked-up product of their highly unsuitable union, and Terence Ian McAdam, the wild brother I haven't seen since I was seventeen. Terry pissed off to Australia; I couldn't blame him really.

I rub some sun cream on Anita's back and give a loud sigh. She turns around to face me.

"Are you okay?"

It seems that girls possess some sort of sixth sense; I'm sure Anita knows just what I'm thinking half the time.

"Sure I am, now I've got you."

"Don't think about the past. Try and forget it and move on."

"It was that family sitting there that did me in; I wished they'd stayed at home."

"We'll make our own family someday. You can give our kids all the love that you like."

"Sorry." I shrug. "Sometimes it still gets to me; the arguing, the drinking, the fights, and the misery of it all. Ian Stuart bloody McAdam; what a fucker!"

"Cheer up. We're sitting here on a beautiful beach, we're engaged to be married on the second of September, and I fancy the pants off you."

I laugh, stand up, and shake the sleep out of my eyes.

"I'm going in for a swim. How about you?"

"Not now I've put all this cream on." Anita shakes her head. "What about a pedalo?"

"Sure; back in a mo and then we can walk over and hire one."

The Mediterranean feels cold on my roasting flesh as I enter the water. I dive under the waves and try to wash off the familiar tendrils of depression that are threatening to grab a hold of me again. No way do I want to go back on the bloody awful Sertraline that I had to take once before; I will have to exercise considerable will-power again and snap myself out of it.

As my body becomes used to the temperature of the water I start to warm up. I surface, float on the waves, and think about the dead girl last seen manacled to my bed who was as fucked up as myself. We should have been true soul mates, but each was secretly looking for that roses-over-the-door ending which the other one was unfortunately unable to provide. Cat was standing in the way of my future happiness with Anita, and had no inclination of ever leaving my flat. Well, she did go eventually, but it was not in the way she had originally intended.

Anita cannot see a small smile playing about my lips as I dive under the surface for a second time. The power and strength that comes with adulthood is often abused. Sometimes there are children who suffer the consequences, but oftentimes it's the adults who have to take the brunt. Dad eventually took the brunt, but Cat had no idea what was coming her way. The look of surprise had still been etched into her features as I had walked back into the bedroom and removed the pillow, ensuring she really *was* dead before making the usual calls to the authorities.

CHAPTER 15

THE COACH STOPS at the next resort, and a giggling crowd of twenty somethings climb aboard. I can see some of them are already pissed, having already sampled large amounts of sangria by the look of it. This is a trip that I've been looking forward to for some time. The middle-agers have all but disappeared, and the night is young. Cala'n Porter is but a short ride away.

I can see the unassuming entrance to the Caves of Xoroi as the coach comes to a halt in the car park. Anita follows my gaze and looks out of the window.

"It's not open yet!"

"It will be." I nod and point to a long queue. "Look at that lot waiting over there."

Anita strains her eyes in the darkness towards what I can make out are a lively crowd of youngsters. As we descend the steps of the coach, the main gate opens and the queue slowly begins to disperse. I grab my girl's hand and run towards the gate.

"Come on; let's party!"

It's a steep climb down. Twinkling lights guide our descent, while the best club sounds can be heard blasting over loudspeakers and drowning out the noise of the sea as it pounds against the rocks to our right. I look about me in awe, while keeping one arm over Anita's shoulders.

"What a great place for a nightclub!"

"Hey look… there's two double beds over there!"

Anita points to a roped off rocky area halfway down to the caves which juts out slightly. Under a canopy sit two king-size beds draped in the finest percale bedlinen. I give a snort of laughter.

"Christ! We can come back up later and have a quick one!"

Anita giggles and shakes her head.

"I don't think use of the beds is part of our entrance fee. We'll probably have to pay extra to lie down on those."

"Oh well, we can have a slow one when we get back to the hotel then."

Inside the cave the first thing I see is a large drinks bar cut out of the rock, and draped with coloured lights. Bar staff are rushing to and fro, serving the mass of people crowded around. Just the other side of a railing the cave is open to the salty elements. Smaller subterranean hollows which are dimly lit lead off the main cave where the bar and DJ are situated, and are filled with tables and benches, mainly occupied. I find us some space on a bench, and whisper in Anita's ear.

"Guard this seat with your life. I'll go and get some drinks in."

"Pimms please." Anita gives me a radiant smile. "Ta."

I wait impatiently for a chance to catch the barman's eye. 'Insomnia' starts up on the turntable, and the DJ cranks up the volume. Suddenly the dance floor behind me is alive with gyrating bodies. I punch the air and shout along with Faithless.

"I can't get no sleep!"

I'm enjoying myself while I wait, but when I take our drinks back to the table I see that Anita's talking to a guy sitting next to her. As soon as she sees me she jumps up, grimacing.

"I'm desperate for a wee. I'll be back in a mo."

As she runs off I can see the guy following her with his eyes. She was showing too much titty and leg for my liking; I'd have to put a stop to that eventually. I slide in next to him, slam the drinks down on the table, and poke him in the ribs.

"Keep your filthy hands off my girl. You speak one more word to her and I'll slit your fucking throat."

The guy's expression changes to one of terror. Without a word he climbs over the bench and is gone, to my eternal delight. By the time Anita returns we have the table to ourselves. She looks along the length of the bench.

"Where have all the people gone?"

"They're dancing." I drain half of the pint of beer in one go. "How about you? Wanna dance with me?"

"Sure!" Anita laughs. "But I can keep it up all night."

"So can I." I leer.

"I bet you can."

We move towards the dance floor. I look around, but the guy who was bothering Anita is nowhere to be seen. I punch the air, grab my girl around the waist, slide my hands down to her bum, and whisper in her ear.

"It's up already. Fancy a session on the beds?"

She hisses a reply; her pretence of disliking the situation is clear.

"Will you stop it? We'll get chucked out!"

The DJ plays a lot of Tiesto stuff. I enjoy flinging my arms about to the mesmerising dance rhythms. Under the coloured lights Anita looks good enough to eat. I give the cave a quick scope as I turn around in time to the beat, and shout in her ear.

"What did that guy say to you while I was getting the drinks?"

"What guy?" She looks blankly at me.

"The guy on our table."

"I don't remember." She shrugs. "I'm not even sure what he looked like, let alone what he said."

"Oh."

I'm momentarily deflated. I'm sure she's lying, because they looked quite cosy to me. Irritated, I turn away from the dance floor and go back to our table, leaving Anita caught up with the music and dancing away on her own. Two brick shit houses are sitting there, and they stare at me as I sit down. One of them fixes me with a gimlet eye and leans over.

"Our little brother says you threatened to slit his fucking throat."

My heart starts hammering away in my chest. I realise I stand no chance against the pure muscle power of these two Neanderthals. I glance over at Anita, who waves at me from the dance floor.

"Well, he's talking out of his arse then, isn't he? He must have got the wrong bloke."

It's a tense moment. I stare them out. The brothers grim move either side of me on the bench, trapping me in my seat. The bigger one pushes his face in my personal space. I want to stick a knife in him. He points to the starry blackness behind the stage, where waves splash up into an area close to the guard rail.

"If I find out you're bothering our brother again this evening, you'll be the other side of that railing over there before you can say *I'm the biggest prick that ever lived*".

Anita comes back. She slides in opposite us and looks questioningly at me. I smile at her, the men stand up and leave, and I swig the rest of my pint to stop my hands shaking. She looks at their retreating backs.

"What did they want?"

"They stopped by to say hello. They went to my school."

"Really?" She looks at me in amazement. "It's a small world!"

You know that intuitive feeling you can get when you know something bad is going to happen? When the club closed and we walked back up to the coach I had just that feeling. I somehow sensed that the two Neanderthals were behind me. I didn't want Anita to get involved, and so I quickly tried to think of a way to get her to walk on ahead.

"I need a piss. I'm going back to the toilet."

She looked surprised.

"I'll wait here for you if you like?"

I shook my head and indicated upwards.

"No, you go on ahead. I'll see you on the bus."

As I turn to go back down again, I'm grabbed around the legs and rugby tackled down onto the rocky steps. Half-pissed teenagers run by in their abarcas and espadrilles, not wanting to get involved. A kick in the side of my chest takes me back to being a kid on the end of one of Dad's drunken beatings. I grab the leg, pick up a piece of glass on the step from a dropped bottle, and ram it into one of the bastard's feet as hard as I can, twisting as I go, while second and third kicks rain down on me from the other one.

Who knows what might have happened if Anita hadn't come back to look for me and intervened? Screaming for help, I see her run over to a couple of security guys who pull the Neanderthals off and help me to my feet. I'll be bruised along the side of my ribs next week, but at least one of them has a hole in his foot the size of a fifty pence piece.

PART 2 – ANITA
CHAPTER 16
JULY 28TH 2000

IT'S THE LAST day of our holiday today. I've had such a brilliant time, apart from that awful night at the caves of course. Poor Paul's quite bruised but is putting on a brave face.

Who would have ever thought that I'd return home engaged to be married? I don't know what Mum's going to say about it, but she seems to like Paul so I don't foresee any problems in that direction.

To finish off we're going for a trip on a glass bottom boat around Mahon harbour. The rep tells us it's the second largest natural harbour in the world. I asked her which one was the largest, and she said Pearl harbour. Paul doesn't seem that interested; in fact I think he wants to go home now and get the wedding underway. Bless him he can't believe his luck I've said yes, and I think he's scared that I'll change my mind. Silly really, but there you are. He's got some hang-ups I think from his childhood which I'm going to work hard in getting rid of. According to Paul he's got the parents from hell; no wonder he doesn't want to invite them to the wedding. He misses his brother as well I think, and blames his parents for Terry going off to Australia. I'm not sure he knows whereabouts his father is actually.

I keep looking at my engagement ring. It's so pretty; lots of silver hearts all joined together in a circle. If I hadn't gone into that pub with my cousins I'd never have met Paul. Fate brought us together, and I can't wait to move into Paul's flat when we're married. It doesn't bother me at all that a girl died in his bed; it wasn't his fault, and he didn't know she was working as a prostitute. Perhaps she was blackmailing one of her clients, and he didn't want his wife to know he was seeing her. I think Paul felt sorry for Catherine and let her stay in his flat because she didn't have anywhere else to go. He's quite kind like that.

I've packed my case and most of Paul's, because otherwise he'd just chuck everything in untidily and wouldn't be able to shut the lid. I can't help but smile as I go into the bathroom to comb my hair and watch Paul stepping out of the shower.

"What a body!" I giggle.

Paul has a quick retort for everything. This time is no exception. He picks up a towel and dries his hair.

"Let's lie down and discuss this."

"Can't; we'll be late for the coach." I check my phone. "It's nearly half past eight and we haven't had any breakfast yet."

"Sod breakfast, I'll eat you instead."

He makes a grab for me, but I jump deftly out of the way.

"You're soaking wet! Hurry up!"

I'm laughing as I slap his backside. Paul sighs and gives me a wink.

"Bugger. I'll eat you later."

I ignore the sheep noises he's making behind me as we join the end of the queue to get onto the coach. I can see Tina and Malcolm ahead of us, and Tina looks around and gives me a wave. They're staying here for another week. I think Paul quite likes Malcom's company; the bar we went to last night with them was a step up from the hotel's entertainment, which is mostly catering for people over fifty. Malcolm's quite funny when he's had a few beers; he starts singing filthy rugby songs in a loud voice and Tina gets horribly embarrassed.

I enjoy learning about places and events. At Mahon harbour the rep gives us each a well-thumbed ticket that serves as our entry onto the boat. Thankfully I can see that the boat is quite a bit bigger than the one at the beginning of our holiday that took us on the snorkelling trip. There looks to be about 200 people on board, and Paul, Malcolm, Tina and I find the last empty seat upstairs in the open air.

The captain starts giving a running commentary about what we're seeing as the boat pulls away. We go past a naval base founded by the British in the 18th century, and Golden Farm, an 18th century colonial house. By now Paul and Malcolm are becoming rather blokey and loud, and aren't listening to the captain at all. To my annoyance they also seem to be ignoring both of us girls and have formed their own little conclave. By the time we get to the 19th century English cemetery used by the American Navy I've given up trying to listen to any more of the commentary, and follow

Tina over to the bar. We buy a soft drink each, look back at the boys telling dirty jokes, and then Tina has an idea.

"Shall we go downstairs to the glass bottom and see what we can see?"

"Sure." I nod in agreement. "I've never been on one of these before."

It's a small area below, with only one other person sitting on the bench; a youngish guy with dark hair probably in his mid to late twenties, who is straining his eyes through the turbulent water. I smile at him and pass the time of day.

"Can you see anything?"

"No. I think we'll see better when the boat stops at the other end of the harbour."

He has a strong London accent. I sit down next to him and peer through the thick viewing windows. Tina sits on the other side of me and shakes her head.

"The boat's churning up all the water."

"Do you want to go back up?" I realise why nobody else has come down yet. "We can come back later."

Tina stands up and moves towards the stairs, and just at that moment I notice that Paul is coming down. I stay seated and wait for him to join me.

"Why are you talking to *him*? What's going on?"

Paul's tone is belligerent and accusing as he points towards the guy seated next to me. I have no idea what he is so angry about, and I shrug.

"I'm not. I just came down to look through the windows with Tina."

"Get up!"

"What? Don't talk to me like that!"

His tone of voice starts to make me angry. The guy next to me stands up and moves towards Paul.

"Hey; no worries! Nothin's goin' on mate."

Paul's hands are bunched into fists. I can't believe what's happening in front of me.

"I'm not your mate. Fuck off!"

"Yeah, I'm goin'!"

As the guy tries to push past Paul in the cramped space to go upstairs, I watch in horror as Paul lashes out and punches the guy on the nose. Immediately I can see blood on the guy's face, who then starts to defend himself and punches Paul hard in the upper abdomen, temporarily winding him. I rush to Paul's aid, who falls to his knees clutching his ribs. The guy wipes blood off his face with his shirtsleeve and disappears upstairs, but not before tossing a remark over his shoulder at Paul.

"You need to see someone, mate. You're not right in the head!"

I'm temporarily reduced to a kind of shocked silence as panting, Paul grimaces and pulls himself up to sit on the bench.

"I'll kill that bastard!"

The scene is like a nightmare, but unfortunately I know it's real. I sit down next to Paul and put my arm around his shoulders.

"Look; I just asked the chap if he could see anything through the window. You've got it all wrong. Tina can vouch for me."

"Just shut up." Paul leans forwards and puts his head in his hands. "I know what I saw."

"You were mistaken." My anger has well and truly risen by now. "I think you owe that guy an apology, and me for that matter. And, just for your information, I can talk to whoever I want to! I wasn't having sex with the guy, just passing the time of day!"

I stand up and make for the stairs, leaving him hunched over and miserable. I don't want to go back upstairs to Tina and Malcolm, and so walk along the bottom deck to the front of the boat, hoping against hope that I don't come across the guy with the bloodied nose. A cooling breeze is welcome on my face, and I stand at the railings fighting back tears. The other passengers leave me alone, and slowly my heartbeat returns to normal.

The boat shudders to a halt and there's a rush to go down to the viewing windows. I've no idea if Paul is still down there or not, and right at that moment I really don't care. I slump down to the decking, curl my legs under me, and look through the railings at the fish swimming about in the clear water. A voice behind me makes me look around.

"I'm sorry; I was a total prick."

I turn back to the fish, trying to ignore him.

"Go away."

To my surprise he disappears without a word, but then returns after five minutes with a cold drink.

"Here; you left your other one downstairs."

"Pity *you* didn't stay down there as well." I take the drink from him. "Thanks."

"I want to be up here with you."

His face is misery personified. I can't get away from him in the confines of the boat, and so give a huge sigh.

"I hope this isn't going to happen every time I make small talk with a member of the opposite sex."

"It won't happen again; I promise. I told you; I was a total prick."

"I'll forgive you this time, but you need to go and say sorry to the guy."

He disappears again. Whether he does apologise I'll never know. Later that evening we make love and he is his usual tender, considerate self. I dismiss the incident on the boat as an aberration in an otherwise perfect holiday.

CHAPTER 17

IT'S DIFFICULT BACKING around a corner at the best of times; it's even worse on the day of your driving test. The examiner is not saying a word as I carry out the manoeuvre. My back is wet with the stress of negotiating through the London traffic, and reversing whilst trying to work out which way to turn the wheel.

"When I tap on the dashboard, please carry out an emergency stop."

It speaks! I drive off down the road, keeping my speed at 29 miles per hour, my heart racing in its anticipation of the examiner's next move. When he hits the dash I slam my foot on the brake, but remember to look in the mirror and signal and then also to look over my right shoulder before pulling away again. I've no idea where I've been driving, but when we turn a corner and end up in the driving centre's car park and I see Mum standing in the shade of a large tree, I'm relieved beyond words that it's over.

"Congratulations, Miss Fairfax, you have passed your driving test."

Yes! I give the thumbs up and a big grin to Mum, who punches the air in delight. I step out of the car, shake the examiner's hand, and follow him inside the centre to complete all the paperwork.

Mum is hopping about from foot to foot as I emerge, blinking in the strong sunlight.

"Well done! I knew you'd pass! What a great birthday present!"

"Thanks for paying for it all." I give her a hug. "I need to text Paul and let him know! Will I be able to borrow the car now?"

"Yes of course." Mum grins at me. "Just let me know when you need it."

Mum drives, as I can't face getting behind the wheel again so soon after my ordeal. I'm beyond happy as we arrive home, knowing that I'll be able to drive up to Gretna on the first of September. Paul will be coming down at the weekend with my birthday present. We'll have a lot of celebrating to do.

"Open your present. You can't wear it yet, but I thought you might like it."

We're alone together in bed; Mum and Dave have gone out for the evening. With a growing excitement I tear off the tissue paper on the small box-shaped parcel.

"Oh God!" I exclaim. "It's my wedding ring!"

Paul looks pleased at my reaction. He reaches over and kisses me on the cheek.

"That's why I didn't let you open it when we were downstairs."

I feast my eyes on the gold band engraved with hearts all the way around, which perfectly resembles my engagement ring. Tears form at the back of my eyes.

"It's beautiful!"

"It's for you, babe."

With trembling fingers I make sure it fits, and then give it back to Paul.

"Keep it for me. I don't want to put it on again until September the second."

"Sure will. You're the only one I'll ever want to wear it."

Paul puts it back into its box, gives me a kiss, and then rolls on top of me.

"I love you so much. I hate being away from you during the week."

"It won't be long until we're together." I return his kiss with passion. "Mr and Mrs McAdam."

The sex act with all its inherent emotions is still relatively new to me, and I enjoy drowning along with Paul in those basic, pleasurable sensations that nobody ever talks about but which I expect are often to the forefront of most people's minds. My fiancée is obviously an experienced lover, but then again he's a few years older than me. I don't want to think about all the girls he's slept with, and he never mentions them. The only one he's ever let on about is Catherine Taylor, but only because he had to at the time due to the police forcing his hand. I don't suppose the mystery of how she died is ever going to be solved.

When our passion is spent I enjoy lying there and feeling the weight of him on top of me. No wonder there's so many people in this world.

I want to do my bit to help out with the cost of the wedding, so without telling Paul I've got myself a little summer job filling shelves at the local supermarket. I've a hunch Paul wouldn't want me to do it, but I like to feel as though I'm contributing and doing something positive to help. It's a laugh actually. All the shelf fillers are students like myself, and although I've only been there three days I've already made friends with Ethan, Kirsty and Will. I saw Kirsty looking enviously at my engagement ring at break time, and I'm enjoying flirting and bantering with Will. I can tell that he finds me attractive, but I don't want to do anything to spoil my relationship with Paul. Will just gets me through the week until payday.

Mum seems okay with the engagement, although she did mention to me that she thinks I'm a little on the young side to get embroiled in a serious relationship. She's spoken to Dad about it, but he's not as keen on Paul as Mum is. I've told both of them that Paul's right for me and he's what I want. I think Dad still worries about who killed Catherine Taylor, but I've told him she had turned Paul's flat into a brothel without his knowledge, and that it could have been any one of the men currently walking the streets of Edinburgh who murdered her.

Will comes up to me as I'm taking jars of jam out of their plastic wrappers. He wants to know if I'll join him and some other students at the pub after work. I want to go, but if Paul rings me and hears lots of background noise he'll want to know where I am. I hesitate, and catch Will looking at my engagement ring. I tell him the truth in that I don't think my fiancée would like it if he found out I was going to the pub with another guy for a drink, no matter how innocent the situation. Will laughs and says forget the fiancée for the evening and turn off the phone. I'm tempted, but at the last minute decline the invitation.

It's now just over two weeks to the wedding. I've earned enough to buy a lovely second hand bridal gown, which is stashed in a box at the bottom of my wardrobe. It's made of ivory coloured silk, and I found it in one of those upmarket charity shops when Kirsty and I went shopping in Camden market last week. Mum would have bought me the best that Harrods could offer, but then the whole family would know that I'm getting married. I've already got just the right pair of strappy sandals to go with the dress, and Kirsty picked me out a fascinator in Debenhams' sale as a wedding present. Paul's ordered flowers for me when I get there, and bless him, has done the majority of the organising. The wedding is set for three o'clock. All I've got to do is borrow Mum's car for the weekend, spirit my wedding dress out of the wardrobe and into the boot, and drive about 320 miles up to Gretna Green. I'll be so excited I won't be able to concentrate on the road, I'm sure.

We've agreed that the day after the wedding Paul will follow me back down to London to tell Mum and Dave and to drop Mum's car off, and then we'll stay with them for a few days before driving back up to see Dad, who has been true to his word and has bought me a car as a combined birthday / passing driving test present. We'll also shift some of my things over to Paul's flat, so that I can move in properly. Paul says he'll tell his mum about the wedding sometime or other, but as he hasn't seen his dad for years I don't think he's in any hurry to let him know about it. Somewhere out there is my mother-in-law, father-in-law and brother-in-law who have no idea that I even exist.

Paul phones me late on the night before I'm due to drive up. He's worried about me finding my way, and wants to go over the route. I tell him I've already looked it up on Google, and inwardly smile at his concern. He takes no notice of my reply and carries on.

"Which road are you taking to get out of London?"

I roll my eyes to the heavens and read from my notes.

"We're in Acton, so I'll get on the A forty." "Then what?"

"Go underneath Hanger Lane gyratory system and get on the M forty"

"To?"

"Oh, stop clucking like a mother hen! I'll find it!"

"To……?"

"Junction sixteen, for Christ's sake!"

Paul gives a chuckle.

"And what's after junction sixteen?"

I'm fuming at his 'I know better than you' attitude.

"I get onto the bloody M twenty five at junction sixteen. Then I sit in a traffic queue for six days and six nights on the M twenty five until I get to junction twenty one, and then I turn off onto the poxy M one going north. Turning off the poxy M one at junction nineteen leads onto the fucking M six. I drive for ten years and then turn off the fucking M six at junction forty five and join the most wonderful B seven oh seven six which goes all the way up to Gretna. See…I'm not a blonde bimbo! And hide yourself in the bathroom when I get there; I'm not supposed to meet up with you before the wedding!"

Paul's rich, throaty laugh echoes all the way down the phone line.

"See you in Gretna, sexy."
And with that he was gone.

CHAPTER 18

"SO YOU'RE PICKING up your new car from Dad and then Paul's driving my car back down?"

I keep my face turned away from Mum, lest she discovers that my eyes are not singing from the same hymn sheet as my mouth. I cover the box holding my wedding paraphernalia with a suitcase, and close the boot.

"That's about it, yeah."

"Phone me when you get to Dad's. I'll worry about you until then."

"I'm alright, okay?" I quash another wave of irritation. "I'm a big girl now."

I wave to Mum as I back off the driveway. If I'm honest with myself I'll admit to feeling more than a little apprehensive as I change into first gear and pull away. Its rush hour, and the momentous journey I now have to undertake weighs heavily on my mind as I ease out onto the Western Avenue. I'm thinking not only about the physical 7 hour trek in front of me, but also of the sudden transition into womanhood that I've rapidly undergone in the past few months; a journey most girls want, but few achieve at such a young age. For the past few days I've been trying to quell the feeling that my life is running on ahead of me faster than I can keep up. Only a few short months before I was a girl attending college without a thought in my head. Now I'm wondering if I should finish the course in Edinburgh or find a job that suits my new grown up status as a soon-to-be married woman.

At Hanger Lane I remember my driving instructor's advice '*in slow, out fast*', keep my cool in the nose-to-tail traffic, and heave a sigh of relief when I eventually turn onto the slip road leading up to the M40. I keep a cruising speed of 70 miles per hour along the motorway, and watch like a hawk for junction 16.

I suspect millions of drivers have turned onto the M25 and suffered a heartsink moment at the sight of the orbital car park in its full nose-to-tail glory. Today is no exception, and four lanes of red tail lights wink at me as I edge along the inside lane. My heart is hammering away in my chest at the sheer number of vehicles. As I start to sweat with anxiety I imagine Paul and I making love in our little Menorcan cave, and by the time I pass under a viaduct displaying the painted epithet '*Give peas a chance*' I'm calmer and actually smiling at the mental imagery of a giant pea trying to roll in-between the cars and dodge the traffic. I relax into the traffic jam, noticing the signs for the M1 as I crawl nearer to junction 17, and decide to switch the radio on. Mum's favourite Radio 3 bursts into life straight away, and I decide to keep with it for its soothing effect.

A car full of twentysomething men edges past on my right side. I try to ignore the tooting horn and lewd remarks shouted in my direction, and focus on Chopin's Nocturne in E flat which I turn up to drown them out. They cut in front of me and turn off for Rickmansworth, and I give them a queenly wave as they go.

It's another half an hour before junction 18 and the turn off to Amersham and Chorleywood comes into view. Fortunately then the traffic begins to pick up speed, and by the time I see signs for the M1 north at junction 21 the concrete of the city has mellowed out into green fields and trees, which are easier on the eye. As I curve round onto the M1 and leave the M25 behind I feel more confident of actually being able to complete the journey without having to call Paul or Dad for help. The thought of having to grovel and admit I am lost does not sit well with me, and to hear Paul constantly telling me 'I told you so' for what will probably be the remainder of our married life is enough to spur me on with renewed vigour and a sense of bold adventure.

Junction 8 to Hemel Hempstead pops up, and my bladder begins to show signs of overfilling. Toddington Services after junction 11 is a welcome sign, especially as Mum had forgotten to fill up with petrol and a red warning light is showing on the dashboard. I pull off the motorway and relish the silence as I turn off the engine. It suddenly occurs to me that I haven't actually ever filled a car up with petrol before, but figure that my bladder is the most pressing of my problems at that precise moment; working out how to use a petrol pump would have to come a close second.

I send Paul a text to say where I am, and then step out of the car. It's a relief to be able to stretch my legs, even though it's only a short walk to the services. Inside the complex it's hot and crowded, with harassed parents shouting at children whining for junk food, and long queues at the restaurant. After locating the washrooms I grab a coffee to take away, and then make my way back to the car. My phone pings with

Paul's reply. I smile as I read his message that he is already waiting for me at the Smiths Hotel. I feel a little tingle of excitement running through my veins.

Never have I felt so utterly humiliated as I stop the car by a petrol pump. Almost at once another driver pulls up behind me, waiting impatiently. I unclip my seatbelt, step out onto the garage forecourt, shrug my shoulders, and look at him reluctantly with what I hope passes for helplessness. He gets out of his car and comes towards me, a man in his late fifties or early sixties. I cringe at the thought of him marking me out as a blonde bimbo, but all I need is to be shown once how to do something, and then I'll learn. I figure that many moons ago whoever he is most probably also had not the faintest idea of how to put petrol in a car. I thank him gratefully as he instructs me in what turns out to be quite an easy procedure. Mum has given me petrol money, and I virtually skip with happiness all the way to the pay desk.

The M1 is running smoothly; Milton Keynes, Northampton, and the Watford Gap services flash by. After junction 18 I pass over the river Avon at Lilbourne and turn off onto the M6, figuring that half of my journey is already over. As I speed past Coventry heading north I suffer a small twinge of regret that Mum will not be with me on my wedding day, and it occurs to me to wonder whether Paul would be willing to go through a church service as well in London for Mum's benefit. It's something that I make a mental note of to ask him about later on.

As all anxiety leaves me I feel hunger pangs gnawing away in my stomach, and pull off the motorway for lunch. I speak to Paul in-between mouthfuls of sausages, chips and peas.

"Hi! I'm at Corley Services on the M six."

He whistles appreciatively in my ear.

"Already? That's about junction three, I think. Well done! Another forty two junctions and a few more hours and we'll be together."

I admit my failings to make him laugh.

"I had to get some old boy to show me how to work a petrol pump."

"Well, now you know for next time." "How much longer have I got d'you think?"

There's a silence, and I can hear the cogs in his head whirring around.

"Oh, about another three and a half hours. You'll be in time for dinner. I've booked a table in the hotel restaurant."

"I'm not supposed to see you today." I chuckle.

"We'll sit on different tables then."

"Have you got my wedding ring?" I gaze idly at my left hand.

"What the fuck d'you take me for? Some sort of mong?" I can't help laughing at him as I say goodbye, finish my meal, and trot back to the car, starting up the engine with more confidence than I've felt all day. I am now of the opinion that once I've completed the journey to Scotland I'll be able to drive anywhere. My new found assurance suffers a minor setback at Birmingham's Gravelly Hill Interchange, but I soldier bravely on up the M6, past Stoke-on-Trent, Liverpool, Manchester, Preston, Lancaster, Penrith, and Carlisle. At the sign for junction 45 I can see the turn off to Gretna. The road is empty, and the landscape is lush and verdant. I start to feel so excited I can hardly sit still, and my gaze keeps shifting from the road to my engagement ring. I turn off the M6 onto the slip road imagining the big day tomorrow; meeting up with Malcolm and Tina again, and watching Paul's face as awestruck, he sees me for the first time in my wedding finery.

My head is saying my wedding vows, but my foot is on the accelerator. When I realise I'm at the end of the slip road and cannot stop in time I say a prayer that no cars might be coming along the B7076 to crash into the side of me, and sail straight over onto what looks like a tiny farm track with a sign saying 'no entry, except for authorised vehicles', and screech to a halt inches away from a locked steel gate.

I close my eyes in relief that Mum's car is still intact. Now all I have to do is somehow turn the car around and get back on the B7076. Gretna beckons, and so does my wedding.

My heart is pounding. On either side there are sheer drops; to my left the bank descends into woodland, and to my right I can see cars down on the M6. Reversing and performing U-turns in a confined space is not my forte, but now I need to call on every scrap of experience I might have gained in manoeuvring a car in order to make it face the opposite direction.

Taking a few deep breaths, I turn the steering wheel to the right, depress the clutch, and slam the gearstick into reverse. In my haste to stop moving backwards and complete the manoeuvre without ending up on the motorway I then engage first gear, but in my state of heightened anxiety I mistake the accelerator for the brake and press down with abandon. The car shoots forward, the front wheels rise up onto a grass verge, and without any warning Mum's dear little Ford Fiesta then plunges down a steep bank. I'm now in full-blown panic as branches slap and scratch the sides of the car as it falls, reaching the bottom of the valley with a terrible crunching sound as the bonnet caves in to an unyielding tree trunk and the engine dies. From the dashboard an airbag inflates, and I feel as though somebody has punched me on the nose.

I sit in shocked silence for what seems like an eternity, shaking and unable to move. I feel wetness on my seat and realise that my bladder has emptied. I try and free my right foot underneath the bent chassis, but my foot and lower leg are trapped. The pressure on my foot is painful. The seatbelt refuses to move when I try and unbuckle it. I realise that I am well and truly stuck.

CHAPTER 19

PINNED BY A buckled chassis and my seatbelt, I look up at the sky through the sunroof, shocked and tearful. To my knowledge nobody had seen me overshoot the junction, and I realise that unless somebody rescues me soon I will not only miss my wedding, but could also eventually die of starvation or dehydration. My handbag containing my phone is stored in the boot, along with a suitcase full of clothes and my wedding outfit. All I have to hand is a small bottle of water and a half-eaten packet of Polo mints.

Desperate to break free, once again I try and dislodge the seatbelt, but to no avail. I wiggle my foot and feel a stab of pain in one of the toes. I try and calm a rising and overwhelming feeling of panic, and take some deep breaths. Apart from a painful foot, a sore nose from the airbag and a sore chest from the seatbelt, I am relatively unharmed and relieved to find that the rest of me still seems to be in one piece. I can move my arms and open the driver's door, but as I cannot exit I close it again.

As the airbag deflates further and the car settles to its new position, I wriggle around in the seat, wet and uncomfortable. I wind down the window and shout out as loudly as I can, but my voice sounds weak and croaky. I take a small sip of water and try again, this time with better results, but only twittering birds respond. I try the hooter and the sound carries mournfully out of the dip, dissipating into the shimmering early-evening heat.

The clock on the dashboard is stuck at four minutes past five. Soon my non-appearance at the hotel will cause Paul to wonder where I am. All I can hope is that he won't think I've changed my mind about the wedding and will contact the police to report me missing. As if on cue I hear the phone ringing in the boot, and count 23 rings before there is silence again.

There is nothing to do but wait. The day is still warm and I need to think coherently. I press my head back against the seat and close my eyes.

The shrill sound of the phone ringing wakes me up. Once again I try to wriggle out of my seatbelt, but I cannot move my right leg. I have no idea of the time, although as it's still light outside I work on the assumption that it's still before 9pm. I have a picture in my mind of Paul pacing up and down the hotel room, wearing out the carpet, and with the phone stuck to his ear. Stuck in my prison I am as helpless as a new-born baby as I mentally will the phone to stop ringing.

Apart from the occasional car rushing past on the B7076 it is eerily quiet. As dusk settles I prepare myself for a night trapped in the car. I suck on a Polo mint in a repetitive bovine-like fashion, my body enjoying the brief burst of sugar which has a strangely calming effect. I take a sip of water, listen to the birds making their preparations for roosting, and wind up the window as the evening cools down; occasionally pressing the horn to no great effect when I hear the sound of passing traffic.

Eventually tiring of wriggling, shouting, honking the horn and tugging at the seatbelt, I press the side of my head to the window and put my faith in providence. As darkness descends there is nothing left to do but think.

I didn't notice him at first in the Rat & Pigeon. That day Esther was celebrating her 19th birthday, and was telling me how I'd be able to get into The Riot House with no trouble at all, but I was still feeling a bit worried about facing the bouncers and getting turned away for being underage. I didn't want to spoil everyone's evening, as I knew my cousins wouldn't leave me outside on the pavement, and would feel obliged to spend the evening with me as I only usually see them when I come up to visit Dad, Tricia and Mandy on college breaks.

I was waiting at the bar with Esther and Elaine, when he asked me if I wanted a drink. I liked the sound of his soft Scottish brogue, and he seemed so shy, blushing away there like a girl. His awkwardness and obvious embarrassment made me giggle. I didn't want to add anything to his discomfiture, especially when Esther started sniggering as well, and so I waited until the other guy he was with had gone to the loo before I plucked up the courage to walk on over. I found his auburn hair and cow-brown eyes appealing, especially his sensuous lips, which truth be told even then I wanted to be pressed onto mine.

He looked at me as if he had just been hit by a thunderbolt, but that's how it was for us, just as it was for Michael Corleone and Appollonia in Mum's favourite movie. As soon as he smiled at me I knew I wanted nobody else.

Esther knew of Paul; she'd often seen him around the pubs and nightclubs, sometimes fighting outside, and sometimes with different girls in tow, but somehow I knew that once he'd met me then we'd be a couple. She told me she usually steered well clear of him, as there was a side to him she wasn't sure of. I told her she was mistaken, and I was all for turning up on time for our first date, but she told me to arrive late; apparently it keeps them keen. I'd only gone out with a couple of boys at college in the past, and so I took her advice. I must say that as soon as I opened the pub door and saw the look of relief in his eyes, I was glad I'd taken Esther's advice.

We hit it off straight away. I wanted to impress him and told him I was an actress; God knows why, I could cringe with embarrassment now at the thought of it. Perhaps at the time I wanted him to think I was more exciting than all the other girls he'd been with, I don't know. However, I am certain of one thing; I was very nervous, and gabbled away just for the sake of it, but nobody stays edgy around Paul for long. Before I knew it we had traded life stories and the evening had ended, although I know I told Paul more about me than he let on about himself. I got the feeling he's not that close to his parents and he kept skirting around the subject, especially where his dad is concerned. In the end I blabbed on about Mum and Dad's divorce, Dad's marriage to Tricia, and the fact that I've now got a step-sister half my age. Paul said he had a brother who lives in Australia. He said it matter-of-factly, and I didn't pick up on any vibes that he actually misses him at all.

Of course Esther was texting even as Dad was driving me back. Tricia raised her eyebrows at me as soon I came in, but I'm skirting around the buddy-buddy relationship. I love Mandy, but Tricia broke up my parents' marriage. I have to get along with her if I'm to keep in touch with Dad, but she's not my mother and never will be. I phoned Esther and told her I'd just been out with the guy I wanted to be with for the rest of my life. Esther snorted down the phone and told me to get a grip. I think she's jealous.

CHAPTER 20

IT'S DARK WHEN I wake up to the sound of the phone ringing yet again. The clock on the dashboard still says four minutes past five. The B7076 is silent, and I figure it's probably the early hours of the morning; the day of my wedding. The heat of the previous afternoon has subsided, although it is still far from chilly.

I try with renewed energy to shift my right leg from under the crumpled chassis, but cannot move it without feeling sharp stabs of pain. I have a feeling one or more toes may be broken, as my foot feels hot and swollen. The thought of having to be married in my trainers causes more tears of self-pity to fall. Eventually I brush them away with my hand; crying will get me nowhere. I sit there, more determined than ever to find a way to free myself when it gets light.

I'm wide awake after my doze. It occurs to me that perhaps my absence may make Paul jump to the wrong conclusion and think that I've changed my mind about the wedding. After seeing his reaction to the poor guy passing the time of day with me on the glass bottomed boat, I feel a tremor akin to fear at a possible backlash which may occur when we eventually meet up again. I tell myself not to be so stupid; Paul would never dream of treating me in the same way. I know he loves me totally, and would move heaven and earth for me if he could.

I wind down the window to have a change of air. Outside I can hear an owl hooting somewhere in the distance, and a slight breeze ruffles the leaves in the trees. It reminds me of that cult Sixties' film 'Blow Up', which was on TV recently. There was a dead body lying in woodland, and the sound the leaves made in the film is what I'm hearing now. It occurs to me as I sit here that it feels quite eerie to hear leaves blowing about in the dark. I don't think I'll ever feel the same way about trees again after this.

I knew there was no way he could be an airline pilot, but I still felt a little disappointed when he confirmed it. He even had the decency to look at me a bit sheepishly at the confession, but hey, ho, at least he's not on the dole. I wonder if he felt I'd let him down when I told him I wasn't an actress? It didn't seem to bother him, in fact he couldn't take his eyes off me. With him I always feel cherished; not many girls can say that of their man.

I didn't care much for sitting in the freezing cold park on that second date and watching his mates play football, but it was nice to be next to him and feel the heat from his body. When he put an arm around me I felt as though I could have sat there all night. I wanted him to kiss me, but when he did it was just a quick peck. Most blokes would have tried to do much more, but bless him, he was a perfect gentleman.

Dad wasn't giving much away when he picked me up. In the past I'd brought a couple of boys home from college to meet Mum, who has always been quite cool about the whole dating thing. However, Dad isn't used to seeing me that often. I get the feeling he wouldn't like any boy I went out with anyway, and tends to treat me as he does Mandy. I asked him what he thought of my new boyfriend, but was not happy to hear Dad's reply that his instinct leaned in the direction of Paul being shifty and unreliable. However, I think as far as Dad is concerned I expect Paul will have to tread barefoot over burning hot nails to prove his love. I'm going to take his opinion with a pinch of salt.

By the third date I was champing at the bit. Dad told me to be careful before dropping me off, but I didn't know what he was so worried about. I wanted to see where Paul lived, and was quite surprised when he came out with a load of excuses not to go there. Of course, knowing what I know now, I realise he must have been worried that I'd come face to face with Catherine Taylor, who as far as we were both concerned at the time, was obviously very much alive. However, apart from briefly seeing someone's pink top hanging up in the hallway before he threw his jacket over it, I had no intuitive thoughts that somebody else shared the flat with him at all. I did wonder about the top though as I made coffee, but figured it could have been left there by any one of his female relatives or friends.

That night will stay with me forever. It wasn't just that later on I'd found out that Catherine had died at the flat earlier that day; actually if truth be told it was more the momentous occasion of me losing my virginity on Paul's settee. It always seemed to me that all the other girls in my class at college were enjoying sex, and it was just boring old me having to lie yet again that I wasn't a virgin. Even though I wasn't planning on returning to that particular college I was pleased to have won the credentials for joining such an elite group, and would definitely enjoy dropping juicy titbits of our moments of passion if the chance ever presented itself in the future, although not the spicier bits.

Some of the girls had let on to me that their first time was disappointing. I can honestly say that we couldn't get enough of each other, and never have I felt so loved and wanted during that transition into womanhood. Mum had Dave, Dad had Tricia, and finally I realised what it was all about; I had someone of my own who found me attractive and wasn't going to leave me, ever. We were inseparable after only a few days.

On that terrible day when I told Paul to fuck off down the phone, and after he was taken in for questioning, I could see by the triumphant look on Dad's face that he knew all his accusatory comments had been justified. Sitting there opposite Paul in the interview room and hearing how he had been living with a prostitute all the time he was with me, made me angrier than hell. I wanted to throw something at him. I had been duped, taken in; somebody for him to use just to satisfy his probably gargantuan sexual appetite. However, once he was able to defend himself I listened and realised that the story he related was making sense. Cat had wormed her way into his flat for her own reasons and gains, and it was Paul who had been used, not myself. Darren had confirmed that Paul had been at work with him at the time Cat was murdered, and never have I been so relieved to be able to apologise to Paul and tell him I still loved him. Dad was convinced Paul was lying through his teeth, but I knew he was wrong and was just trying to save face and pride.

Darkness is absolute, and the hour of my wedding moves nearer and nearer as the night progresses. I vow to start honking the horn as soon as it gets light and I hear any sounds from the road. Nobody would be able to see me trapped down in the foliage undercover of night, and to be quite honest, who would be walking about now on the B7076? I reason my best chance is to be discovered by an early-morning dog walker or a car which has stopped for some reason or other.

I need another wee. The seat is still wet and so I just let it go; there's no other way around it. I take another sip from my bottle of water, and break out another Polo. I toot the horn just for the sake of it, to no avail. I resign myself to a night trapped in the car.

Paul's definitely got charm; he won Mum over straight away. I knew Dad would have been on the phone to her about him, but bless her, Mum waited to meet Paul before making up her own mind. I know she would have voiced any concerns to me as soon as he left for home, but all she said was how thoughtful he had been in asking her permission to take me on holiday. I wish she hadn't gone on about contraception though and embarrassed him, but that's Mum; straight to the point and no frills.

It would be nice to meet Paul's parents, but it doesn't look as if that will happen any time soon. I don't even know where they live, and Paul usually changes the subject if I start asking about his mum and dad. As far as I can gather his dad is an alcoholic who left the family some time ago, and who I think might be violent when he's drunk. However, surely he can't be trollied all the time? Wouldn't he like to meet his new daughter-in-law? What's Paul's mum like? I'm sure that if I got to know my future in-laws I would learn a whole lot more about Paul. Sometimes he's like a closed book; we could have just made love, but if you ask the wrong question, even when he's in a good mood, he disappears behind the high wall he's built around himself.

I suddenly remember the happy family scene on the beach, and Paul calling his father 'Ian Stuart bloody McAdam'. It occurs to me that I might be able to look up the name online and see if that leads me anywhere. I might even find both of them still living in Edinburgh. It would be great to turn up on their doorstep!

Will I die down here? The answer comes back a big, fat NO! Already

I expect Paul has contacted the police and also my mum to tell her I never arrived, and I reason that sooner or later somebody is going to find me. Just for the sheer hell of it I try and start the engine, but am not too surprised when nothing happens. I determine to put battle plans into place at first light.

I open the car door. Freedom is a few tempting steps away. Something scurries past in the undergrowth, and I slam the door shut again.

I yawn and think back to the previous week and Cat's photo and the article about her in the Edinburgh Standard that Dad had sent down to Mum. She'd hidden it quite well, but I'd managed to find it in her 'not-so-secret drawer' at the back of her bureau. In the past I'd found lots of things in there that I was not supposed to find, and when I discovered the clipping it irked me no end to think that Dad was trying to get Mum on his side and turn her against Paul. Mum had not yet said anything to me about it, but I knew it was only a matter of time.

The article had been written after Cat's parents had offered up twenty thousand pounds as an incentive in finding their daughter's killer. Paul had mentioned the reward in passing, but obviously couldn't claim the money as he had no more information to give.

I remember thinking at the time that Cat's parents looked quite well off. Her father Thomas was an insurance broker, and her mother Ann a midwife. I still failed to see even as I re-read it in my mind how a daughter of Thomas and Ann could have possibly stooped so low as to become a homeless prostitute, grabbing money wherever and whenever the opportunity arose. I could only assume that perhaps she had fallen out with her parents and left home without any qualifications or funds to her name.

Who had murdered Cat? Was it a customer after a sex game had gone wrong? Had Cat turned to blackmail? Had there been a man in the wardrobe taking pictures? Whoever it was it could not have been Paul, as he was at work that afternoon. I vowed not to let Dad carry on besmirching Paul's good name with Mum. It just wasn't fair.

CHAPTER 21

AT LAST DAWN begins to break. Twittering birds begin to greet the new day, and I open up the car's window to listen out for signs of life. I am hungry, thirsty, and stink to high heaven of urine. A few cars pass by on the Gretna road, and I start to honk the horn in a frenzied fashion. In-between pressing down on the hooter my ears suddenly pick up the noise of a dog barking from somewhere up above. This sound is music to my ears; where there is a dog, there is usually an owner. I press the horn continually, and to my delight I look to my right a few moments' later and a collie's limpid brown eyes are staring at me through the side window. Two paws scratch the glass.

"Hello!" I croak, and wind down the window. "Am I glad to see you!"

I stroke the warm face, and could cry at the sight of another life form. Pretty soon there is the sound of boots tramping down through the woodland, and somebody calls the dog back and puts him on a lead. A man possibly a farmer and in his late fifties comes up to me and looks in through the open window.

"Are you okay?"

"Not really." I sigh. "I can't get out. The seatbelt is jammed, and my foot's trapped."

"Not to worry." He pulls a mobile phone out of his pocket. "There's not much signal in this dip; it's coming and going. I'll just go up to the main road and phone for an ambulance. I'll be back in a minute."

"Could you please get my phone out of the boot?" I cannot seem to stop my eyes from welling up. "I might have some signal, because it's been ringing. I need to phone my fiancée. It's our wedding day today."

"Good God!" The man goes around to the back of the car. "You are in a pickle, aren't you?"

"Thanks so much!" I take the phone from his hand and see I have one bar of signal, which seems strong enough for the moment. "I'll try and call Paul from here. If not, could you call him when you come back?"

"Sure. I'm not going to try to move you in case you've broken any bones, but we'll have you out of there in no time. What's your name?"

"Anita. Anita Fairfax."

"Don't you worry, Anita; everything's going to be okay."

My saviour and his canine friend disappear back into the trees. I look at the time on my phone; 05:48. I press Paul's number and he answers immediately.

"Where the fuck are you?"

He sounds angry; angrier than I've ever known him to be. Suddenly I can't stop crying, and my words come out disjointed by hiccups and grief.

"I've h-had an accident! Somebody's just f-found me! I — I've been trapped in the car all night just outside Gretna!"

"And you've only just phoned me *now*? I've been ringing you all fucking night for God's sake!"

He sounds crazed; like a madman. There is no reasoning with him, and no sympathy for my plight. I'm shocked, and rendered speechless.

"Answer me!"

The aggressive, almost inhuman tone of his voice is completely foreign to what I would have expected from a worried fiancée. I end the call and turn off the phone completely to block him out.

Within a few moments the collie is panting at the window again, and its slightly overweight owner is carefully re-negotiating the slippery undergrowth, now wet with dew.

"Ambulance is on its way, and also a fire engine to cut you out. I'll stay up on top to make sure they know where you are."

"You've been so kind. Thank you." I look up at him out of the window. "I don't even know your name."

"Hamish Rennie; pleased to be able to help."

"Thanks Hamish, I'm very grateful to you."

"No problem; I'll go and wait for the ambulance."

While Hamish goes up onto the road, I quickly turn on my phone again and call Mum to give her the sad news about her car. I can hear her sigh of relief over the airwaves.

"Paul phoned me last night when you didn't turn up at his flat. Where are you, and more importantly, how are you? Paul said he'd report you as missing. We've been so worried!"

"My foot will need some treatment, but I'm okay. It's your car that's not." Tears well up in my eyes again. "I'm so sorry; I overshot a junction and ended up down a bank. The front end is crumpled; it hit a tree. I'm just outside Gretna Green. Someone's just called for an ambulance for me."

"Don't worry about the state of the car; it's why we pay insurance premiums. Did you take a wrong turning then? Why are you at Gretna?"

In my haste to reassure my mother, I had completely forgotten that she did not know the reason for my detour."

"I…er….came off at the wrong junction on the M six. I was getting tired."

"Just as long as you're okay; that's all that matters.

"I'm just going to hospital as a precaution. I've wet myself; I couldn't get out of the car to do a wee."

"Don't worry; the paramedics have come across worse things than that." Mum's voice is reassuring. "I'll phone Dad now. He'll know the nearest hospital to you with an Accident and Emergency department. He'll meet you there."

"Thanks Mum."

I have a little cry of relief as Mum clicks off. Just as I go to turn off the phone it rings again. I look at the incoming number, decline to answer, and activate the off switch.

Why on earth was Paul so angry with me? His odd reaction to my plight has caused the first seedlings of doubt to flower in my mind. Has Dad's opinion of Paul been correct all along?

My head is awash with confusion as I await the emergency services' arrival. Should I really be going ahead with this wedding? Why is Paul not close to his parents? Does he have anger management issues? If he does, then there's a burning question which needs to be answered; what really happened to Catherine Taylor?

Before long the quiet woodland is awash with paramedics and firemen with noisy cutting equipment. Mum's car deteriorates further and I hear a sickening crunching of metal as the chassis is cut away to free my foot, which when exposed is swollen and painful. When my shoe is cut off I can see bruising and swelling to the front of the foot and to three toes. The medical team are kindness itself, and expertly apply splints to two of the toes which I'm informed are probably broken. Wet and embarrassed and hooked up to a glucose drip, I am then lifted up the bank on a stretcher and deposited unceremoniously in the back of an ambulance with all my belongings. When the ambulance moves off and I find out that we are heading for Cumberland Infirmary, I send Dad a quick text and ignore the seven already on the display screen from Paul.

CHAPTER 22

I'M LYING ON a trolley in A&E's Triage area, and I can hear some sort of disturbance outside in the waiting room. Presently a flushed and harassed nurse bursts through the swing doors.

"Anita, we have your fiancée at the reception desk. Would you like him to wait with you?"

Before I have a chance to reply, the doors swing open for a second time and Paul crashes in, strung out with worry and red-eyed through lack of sleep.

"Anita, I'm so sorry I was angry with you!" Panting, and immune to A&E protocol, Paul grabs my hands with both of his own. "I thought you'd changed your mind about the wedding! I'm so glad you're okay!"

The nurse retreats back into Reception, and I am left looking up at Paul. His anxiety and concern are obvious. In fact I feel a little guilty now for turning my phone off and ignoring him. However, I keep my voice cool and make him suffer.

"Paul, I spent all night trapped in the car. My phone was in the boot, and I couldn't reach it."

"Yes I realise that now; I'm such a prat.   Please forgive

me, I was so worried I didn't know what I was doing. I've been phoning every bloody A&E unit in the area!"

His earnest face and beseeching eyes boring into mine make me feel sorry for causing him so much heartache. I give his hands a squeeze.

"You're forgiven. If they let me out of here we might even have time to get married. My wedding dress is over there in the corner." I point to a box, a suitcase, and a bag of wet clothes taking up space. "If I can't wear any shoes I'll go barefoot."

I smile up at him and see relief soften his features.

"Even in your hospital gown you're beautiful."

His contrition is absolute. I feel a total heel for being angry with him.

"I've just got to be assessed and have an x-ray, and then hopefully I'll be able to go if they can treat my foot soon."

"We've still got another six hours. I'll tell them it's our wedding day and perhaps they'll put a spurt on it." He grins at me. "We'll make it! I love you so much!"

He leans over and kisses me. It's lovely to feel wanted.

Dad finds us as I'm being wheeled to X-Ray. Paul stays silent as Dad and I talk. I'm aware of some tension between the two of them, and as we wait for a radiographer Dad asks Paul to leave so that he can speak to me in private. I hope against hope that Mum hasn't told him where I was found. As Paul reluctantly moves outside into the corridor, Dad wastes no time in beating about the bush.

"Mum told me you were found close to Gretna Green."

Dad's voice is brusque and business-like. I know this from old; it means he's moving in for the kill.   I shrug my shoulders and sigh.

"I already told Mum; I got lost and took the wrong turning off the M six."

"But that's miles out! Are you getting married to him? Is that why you were found near Gretna? If you are, think again my lovely; he's not for you. You're eighteen years old with your life ahead of you. Don't throw it all away on *him*!"

You can always trust Dad to speak his mind. I dredge up all the acting lessons I've ever had, and keep my eyes on the doorway.

"You're barking up the wrong tree, Dad; honestly."

"I do hope so." He sounds resigned. "It's in the Standard that the police are following up hundreds of leads on Catherine Taylor's killer, now there's a twenty thousand pound reward."

"Yes I know." I shrug again. "She was a prostitute, using Paul's flat to take clients back to without his knowledge. It was probably one of her customers who murdered her; we'll never know I expect."

"Oh, we'll know soon enough." Dad's voice is grim. "I'm keeping my ear to the ground on this one."

Unfortunately I know only too well that he will be. I also know that I'll never hear the last of it now. I change the subject quickly as Paul marches back in and silently plonks himself down next to me.

"Thanks for buying me the car, Dad. I'll stay with Paul and recover for a couple of days, and then we'll come over and pick it up."

"My pleasure." Dad looks grimly at Paul. "I'll speak to Mum and sort out getting her car over to the loss adjusters for you."

As soon as Dad is out of range foraging for food, I whisper to the A&E staff that I'm getting married at three o'clock. They turn into kindness personified and speed up my discharge. With my toes strapped up and the ball of my foot off the ground in a strange-looking type of shoe, I am let out on the advice to rest and keep my foot elevated as much as possible. Dad and Paul battle it out between them regarding where I should recuperate as they help me into a wheelchair, but I have no intention of letting Dad win on that one. It's my wedding day, and my place is with my fiancée. Dad's face is as black as thunder as he drives off, doubtless cursing Paul's reflection in his rear-view mirror as soon as he's alone. Paul mutters under his breath as the Audi pulls away.

"What *is* the matter with that guy? Why does he always look as though he's got a rod stuck up his arse?"

I suppress the urge to giggle as I climb into his car.

"He'll come around in time. I think it's the father-daughter thing. He can't bear to think that he isn't number one in my life anymore."

I'm getting really good at lying, because Paul seems to accept my explanation. As he loads all my bags into the boot and sends the wheelchair shooting across the car park with a well-placed kick, he gives a self-satisfied smirk.

"Well, he'd better get used to it. *I'm* flavour of the month now!"

There isn't much time to prepare. In our room at the Smiths Hotel I'm riding high on being rescued in time for our nuptials. Malcolm and Tina have sent a text to say that they've arrived and are looking around the gift shop. I don't even care that I'm in pain and it's unlucky to see the groom before the wedding; I'm eager to start the next stage of my life as Mrs Anita McAdam.

Paul holds me close when I come out of the bathroom in my wedding finery, and tells me I'm the most beautiful person inside *and* out, who has ever lived. I feel loved, cherished, and fit to burst with happiness.

The long silk gown hides the fact that I'm wearing one orthotic shoe and one strappy sandal. Holding Paul's arm I hobble out of the hotel foyer at ten minutes to three to loud clapping and cheers from the staff on reception, and walk across to the Old Blacksmith's Shop opposite, with Tina and Malcolm in tow. This is my big day, and I'm going to make the most of it.

There's nothing upmarket about the Old Blacksmith's Shop; it is what it says it is. I look around the shop while the registrar and his aide get their paperwork together. By the age of the wooden rafters adorned with horseshoes above, I surmise the place must be at least a couple of hundred years old. Taking pride of place in the middle of an old barn-like structure is the good luck anvil with its ceremonial hammer, over which thousands of couples over the years have joined hands and said their vows. Up a few steps to the back of the shop is a worn-out looking pair of bellows on the floor, and several rusting blacksmiths' tools.

I can see four chairs present; two either side of the anvil and two behind. The registrar bids Paul and I to sit in the two front seats, and Tina and Malcolm take the chairs to the rear.

I look around at Tina sitting behind me, and give her a nervous grin. She gives me a thumbs up in reply. Paul, pale and serious, sits quietly waiting for the service to begin, lost in his own little world.

The registrar rises up from his table and comes to stand in front of us, and an adrenaline rush causes my heart to step up its rhythm.

"Good afternoon ladies and gentlemen, and welcome to the Old Blacksmith's Shop, Gretna Green, for the marriage of Paul Christopher McAdam and Anita Melody Fairfax. I am Keith Hutchinson, Registrar, and sitting behind me is Adrian Childs, who will be recording the proceedings."

The registrar clears his throat before continuing.

"I must first of all mention that this place in which we have met has been duly sanctioned according to law for the celebration of marriages, and if any person present knows of any legal reason Paul Christopher McAdam and Anita Melody Fairfax should not be joined in matrimony, then they should declare it now."

I wait for Mum or Dad to rush in at the last moment voicing protestations, but nothing happens. Tina and Malcolm are silent, and so the registrar carries on.

"Paul McAdam has chosen a reading of Seamus Heaney's poem '*Scaffolding*' today."

I look sideways over the anvil at Paul, who returns my gaze with a smile. I haven't come across '*Scaffolding*' before, and listen with interest as the registrar reads from a sheet of paper.

'Masons, when they start upon a building, are careful to test out the scaffolding;
Make sure that planks won't slip at busy points,
Secure all ladders, tighten bolted joints.
And yet all this comes down when the job's done

Showing off walls of sure and solid stone.
So if, my dear, there sometimes seems to be
Old bridges breaking between you and me,
Never fear. We may let the scaffolds fall
Confident that we have built our wall."

I have a sudden mental image of a high brick wall; on one side are Paul and I, and on the other is the rest of the world. It's a scary thought, and one on which I don't care to dwell.

When the poem comes to an end the registrar folds the paper and smiles at us.

"Will the bride and groom please stand."

My legs are definitely shaking, even my little posy of wildflowers is quivering. Keith Hutchinson focuses on Paul.

"Paul Christopher McAdam, will you take Anita Melody Fairfax to be your lawful wedded wife, to be loving, faithful and loyal to her for the rest of your married life?"

Paul looks deep into my eyes.

"I will."

"And Anita Melody Fairfax." The registrar's booming tone almost makes me jump out of my skin. "Will you take Paul Christopher McAdam to be your lawful wedded husband, to be loving, faithful and loyal to him for the rest of your married life?"

I nod and smile at Paul.

"I will."

"Please sit." Keith Hutchinson turns over his piece of paper. "In the absence of any requested songs, I hope you'll both take a minute to listen to another reading; this time to one of my favourite poems. The author is unknown."

'A good marriage must be created.

In marriage, the little things are the big things. It is never being too old to hold hands.

It is remembering to say 'I love you' at least once a day.

It is never going to sleep angry.

It is having a mutual sense of values and common objectives.

It is standing together and facing the world.

It is forming a circle of love that gathers in the whole family.

It is speaking words of appreciation and demonstrating gratitude in thoughtful ways.

It is having the capacity to forgive and forget.

It is giving each other an atmosphere in which each can grow.

It is a common search for the good and the beautiful.

It is not only marrying the right person

– It is being the right partner.'

The words have a distinct meaning for me. As I sit there on a well-worn chair in the dust of the little blacksmith's shop I am one hundred per cent certain I am marrying the right person, and that my love for Paul will be enough to change his somewhat bizarre, but thankfully infrequent, tendency to aggression.

The registrar lets the words sink in a little further, bids us to stand, and then turns towards Paul.

"Paul, please repeat after me, I do solemnly declare that I know not of any lawful impediment why I, Paul Christopher McAdam, may not be joined in matrimony to Anita Melody Fairfax."

Paul's reply echoes loudly around the blacksmith's shop, and I feel a little tingle of excitement travel down my spine as I make my own declaration. Then acting on the registrar's prompt, he then reaches over the anvil and places the band of golden hearts on the trembling third finger of my left hand, and steadies both of my hands with his own.

"I give you this ring as a token of our married life together. I call upon these persons here present to witness that I, Paul Christopher McAdam, take you Anita Melody Fairfax to be my lawful wedded wife, and to be loving, faithful and loyal to you until death do us part."

With superb self-restraint I manage not to cry as I blurt out my own vows and give Paul a plain gold ring. Keith Hutchinson picks up the ceremonial hammer, gives us a big grin, pronounces us husband and wife, and brings the hammer down upon the anvil, ending my 18 years of spinsterhood. I am now Mrs Anita McAdam.

CHAPTER 23

"DO YOU THINK it's a good idea? He hates my guts!"

"It'll be fine. Dad will come round; don't worry."

"We'll go on the bus then after dropping the cases off at my flat, and I'll drive your new car back."

"It's *our* flat." I waggle my forefinger at him in mock outrage. "I'm looking for work now to help with the costs, don't forget."

Paul comes over and kisses me.

"Whoops; force of habit. Yes, of course it's our flat. Do you really want to give up college?"

"Yeah." I nod. "It's a waste of time; I'd rather be earning."

"There might be a vacancy at Dodd's in the offices." Paul gives me a squeeze. "I'll ask tomorrow."

After a wonderful night spent consummating our marriage, it's now time to leave the Smiths hotel and face reality. I hobble about packing cases and trying to quell a growing unease at the thought of having to tell my father that not only are we now in a state of wedded bliss, but that also I'm going to give up college and look for a job.

Tricia sees us walking down the road, and is at the door before we've reached the gate.

"Well, hello! This is a surprise!" She smiles at me, eyes Paul up and down, and extends her right arm towards him. "You must be Paul; I'm Tricia."

"Hi." Paul shakes Tricia's hand and stands there silent and rooted to the spot as Tricia checks me over.

"Come in, come in! Your dad will be so pleased to see you? How's the foot?"

"It's okay." I grimace. "A bit of pain, but I'll be as good as new in a few weeks."

"Glad to hear it. Mike! Anita and Paul are here!" Mandy

runs out to greet us instead, but hides behind

Tricia at the sight of Paul. Paul, well prepared in advance for meeting my step-sister, produces a bag of chocolate buttons from his pocket and waves it in the air.

"A little bird told me that somebody here might like chocolate?"

Mandy peeps out from behind Tricia's legs and smiles.

"I do."

"I double-dare you to come over here!"

Paul's smile wins Mandy over, and she runs to him, grabs the chocolate, and runs back to Tricia. We're all laughing as Dad comes out into the hallway.

"Hi; I suppose you've come for the car?"

Dad's voice is unusually cool as he looks at the two of us standing there. I'm momentarily lost for words, and suddenly decide to get it over with straight away.

"Hi Dad. Yes please, but also to tell you that Paul and I were married yesterday. You'll be seeing more of me, as I've now moved into Paul's flat in Hayes Road."

I wait to be struck by lightning, but nothing happens straight away. Instead, Dad stands there in shock, silent as a statue and no doubt fuming impotently. To add salt to the wound, I deliver a final *coup de grace.*

"*And* ….I'm not going back to college. Paul thinks there might be a job for me at Dodd's where he works."

Dad ignores Paul and looks at me, open-mouthed. His total indifference to my husband starts to make me angry. When at length he speaks, it's a kind of relief.

"Does Mum know all this?"

"No, not yet, but I expect you'll tell her as soon as we're out the door, which by the looks of it won't be too long."

My new husband, to his credit, has stayed silent. However, as Dad turns and walks away, Paul, hands bunched into fists by his side, lashes out with his tongue.

"Hey! You're fucking rude! D'you know that?"

Immediately Tricia and Mandy run upstairs, while Dad swings around, eyes blazing, and squares up to his new son-in-law. Sensing danger, I step in-between them.

"I'm sorry if I've upset you. We're off now; I'll come back some other time for the car."

With a sigh, Dad takes a keyring out of his pocket, pulls one of the keys off, and gives it to me before going up the stairs to Tricia.

"It's the blue one in the driveway."

I'm crying as I virtually push Paul out of the door, desperate to be away. In the driveway stands a brand new metallic blue Honda Civic, but I realise my orthotic shoe will make driving impossible. Tearfully I give the key to Paul and climb inside, who starts up the engine and screeches off in true *Starsky and Hutch* style before I've even fastened my seatbelt.

"Slow down! Don't crash the thing before I've even had a chance to drive it!"

"Slow down?" Paul's face is contorted in rage as he presses down harder on the accelerator. "You're *telling* me to slow down?"

"Yes! For Christ sake slow down!" The words, unheeded, come out in a kind of sob. "Stop! Stop the car! I want to get out!"

"Nobody tells me to do anything!"

Terrified and beyond tears, I pray for the sight of a police car, but to no avail. Wild with anger, Paul accelerates through the back streets at an alarming rate, only slamming on the brakes when he has to join a line of vehicles waiting at a junction. Seizing my chance I unbuckle my belt, grab my bag, open the car door, and hobble onto the bus in front of us in the queue as fast as my broken toes will allow. I've no idea where the bus is going, but the relief of getting away from him is overwhelming. Shaken, I ignore stares of surprise from the other passengers, and take a seat where I can look out of the back window. To my horror, instead of turning right at the junction towards our flat, Paul screeches left in a cloud of smoke and begins to follow the bus, shooting me evil looks whilst keeping three inches from its exhaust pipe.

I pay the conductor the maximum fare and move away to the front, remembering with a feeling of exaltation that sooner or later it will stop on one of the green bus-only lanes to pick up passengers, and that Paul will have to drive on or face a fine. However, my relief is short-lived. When the bus stops I am dismayed to hear a commotion behind me. I look around in horror to find that Paul has pushed himself to the head of the passenger queue and is striding down to the front of the bus and pointing in my direction.

"You! Get off! Now!"

"Go away!" I look around desperately for help. "Fuck off!"

A guy who would not look out of place on a rugby pitch stands up behind me and blocks Paul from coming any nearer.

"You heard the lady. She said fuck off!"

Paul realises he's met his match with the prop forward, who then pushes him unceremoniously off the bus to loud applause. Looking behind through the back window I can see my Honda Civic parked in a Greenways lane, and a burly warden awaiting Paul's return. I thank the guy, and sink down in the seat, mortified with fear and embarrassment.

It's another hour before the bus reaches St. Andrew's Square terminal at the end of its route. By then I've received countless calls and texts of apology from Paul professing his undying love, none of which I've bothered to answer. As I exit the bus I'm miserable, dejected, and desperately want to phone Dad, but pride gets in the way. I'm down to my last couple of pounds, and have no way of getting back to the flat, not that I want to go there anyway.

I hobble to a seat, stumped and wretched; angry at Paul, at my dad's reaction to the marriage, and at the world in general. Mum sends a text and says she's spoken to Dad but forgives me for marrying without her knowledge, and I'm grateful for that. She hopes my foot is okay. I text and tell her I will ring soon, apologise for ruining her car, and tell her that I will visit as soon as I can. I wanted to call and hear her voice, but I need to be able to speak to her when I'm more in control of my emotions.

Meanwhile Paul is ringing and ringing the phone like a mad person, but when he calls again for the umpteenth time I see red, accept the call, and screech down the line like a banshee.

"For fuck's sake leave me alone!"

Paul's voice, sounding just like calmness personified, answers straight away.

"Thank God! Where are you?"

He sounds as normal as normal can be. Perplexed at the mercurial change of mood, I test him out further.

"Sitting in a bus station."

"Which one?"

"What do you care? Piss off."

"I'll come and get you if you tell me where you are."

"No; I'm going to phone Dad in a minute, because I don't know what you'll do when you find me."

This is true. He could be seething; white hot with anger and just masking it. I have absolutely no idea.

"I'm sorry about earlier, I was an absolute shit. Your dad got my back up. I'm sorry I took it out on you. Please tell me where you are."

I'm tired, in pain, and I've had enough. Only fear keeps me rooted to the spot.

 "No, leave it for tonight." I sob. "I can't take any more." I'm still in tears hours later when he pulls up beside me in the car, having driven around all the bus terminals in the city. He leaps out of the car, puts his arm around me and hugs me tight, saying the words I am longing to hear."

"I'm so sorry. Let's go home and start again."

I can do nothing else at that point except agree with him.

CHAPTER 24

DODD'S DO INDEED have a vacancy for a clerk, and I'm sure it's only down to Paul's charm and persuasion that I manage to secure the post. I know nothing of office work, invoicing or month-end figures, but I'm fortunate in being a quick learner. After only a few weeks I'm on the ball with the invoicing, filing and letter typing, but still working with a very patient Diane on producing the month-end profit/loss figures. Diane's a lovely grandmotherly type who's decided to retire early. I only hope that I don't make a complete balls-up of it all once she's gone.

It's one of those old fashioned family companies where anybody aiming for the top of the mountain will find the boss's son is already there, and surprisingly enough that he hasn't passed one other soul on the ascent. That said, they do look after their staff very well. I'm accepted immediately into the clan on Paul's recommendation. Old Mr Dodd still has the antiquated system in place of clocking in and out at lunchtimes and at the start and end of each day, although it's Flexi-time and he's happy just as long as 35 working hours are showing at the end of each week. It suits us, because if we have to work an extra hour's overtime then we can leave an hour earlier on another day of our choosing in the same month, although it's taken for granted that staff won't run up hours of overtime and then zip off to the continent for a fortnight. Mr Dodd always checks that staff have clocked out at lunchtimes, which is fair enough I suppose. It's quite a good system actually.

I soon find it's one of my irksome duties to check that all 70 members of staff have worked the required amount of hours before authorising their weekly pay. Checking the clocking system is time-consuming and takes me away from other duties. However, as far as the staff are concerned, it's the most important job in the whole factory.

Paul and I save on petrol by starting work at the same time and travelling together in one car. Sometimes if I know Paul has to work late I'll take mine, but usually he'll only stay later if there's a rush job on.

I'm getting to know Darren; a name I've only heard Paul mentioning in passing before. Darren Maynard is a laugh a minute. He's one of life's 'duckers and divers' as they say down in London; the first to pick up anything that's 'fallen off the back of a lorry'. He brings all the worksheets to me for invoicing, and he's the type who always has a quick retort for any remark. Sometimes I find the work a bit boring, and look forward to Darren's arrival with the worksheets for a quick bit of banter and light relief. I'm aware that he finds me attractive, but he's always careful not to overstep the mark. After all, I'm a married lady.

I'm slaving over a hot word processor late in November when Darren pops his head around the office door.

"Hi! Got some more worksheets for ya!"

I look up and smile at him.

"You know what you can do with your worksheets, don't you?"

"Ouch!" Darren winces and crosses his legs. "Now that's not very nice."

Chuckling, he steps into the office, closes the door, and waves a pile of papers in my direction.

"Don't say I never give you anything."

Unimpressed, I yawn and take them off him.

"Cheers; you're a brick."

An expression of pseudo-annoyance passes over Darren's features.

"A prick?"

"No!" I exclaim. "A brick!"

Darren laughs and feasts on me with his eyes.

"How are you doing in the new job?"

"Oh, I'm getting the hang of it now." I nod. "Thanks to Diane; she taught me a lot before she retired."

"She hated checking the clocking records, I remember that."

I put the worksheets in my in-tray and look up from the desk.

"I don't like that job either; it takes ages."

Darren stands in front of me, unwilling to leave. I'm not keen on him staying too long in case Mr Dodd or Paul notices. I clear my throat.

"Well, I've got work to do even if you haven't……"

Darren takes the hint. At the door he turns around quickly.

"How long do you keep them for?"

"Keep what?" I look at him blankly.

"The clocking records."

"Oh; just for that particular financial year." I shrug. "There's no space to keep them for any longer than that."

"So you've got them from January then?"

"Yeah."

He disappears, I look back at the word processor, and within moments forget he was ever there in the first place.

Soon the December chills are upon us, but Paul and I are getting on like a house on fire. True, I now know how to avoid upsetting him, but one Sunday morning near Christmas after an energetic and mutually satisfying lovemaking session, I decide to throw a spanner in the works while he's in a good mood.

"I'd like to invite your parents to the flat for Christmas dinner."

I roll over on top of him while he thinks about an answer. I lay my head on his chest and roll one finger over the top of his nipple. Immediately his body stiffens, but it's not through lust.

"Why?"

His voice is curt as he pushes me off him and sits up. Undaunted I carry on.

"We've been married over three months, and I still haven't met them. Don't you think that's peculiar? We're going to see my Mum on Boxing Day; I'd like to meet yours."

"For fuck's sake! You won't let it rest, will you?"

I'm aware that I've pissed him off now, so I mentally shrug my shoulders, have a quick re-think, and change tack.

"Are you ashamed of me then? Will they think I'm not good enough for you?"

He leaps out of bed like a mad thing.   Naked, he starts

pacing backwards and forwards across the bedroom carpet.

"Okay! Get your clothes on; we're going there now!"

Surprised, I get up and stand in his way.

"What? Now? They won't know we're coming!"

"You want to go there; then we'll go!"

He starts rooting through drawers looking for clean clothes. With a growing feeling of apprehension I make my way to the bathroom to get showered and dressed. He's waiting by the front door with his car keys as I walk down the hallway to the kitchen.

"Let me have a cup of tea first! Do you want one?"

"No."

His agitation is beginning to make me uneasy as I swallow a plate of Weetabix and a cup of tea in record time. I don't bother washing up, but follow him out to the car.

"If you drive like a maniac I'll jump out at the next set of traffic lights."

I slide into the passenger seat, buckle my belt, and pray for a smooth ride. Within a short while we're heading out onto the M8.

"Where do they live?"

"Glasgow. It'll take about an hour. But it's only Mum living there; Dad pissed off years ago. Will you be satisfied then?"

"Yes."

He keeps to the regulation 70 miles per hour, and is unusually silent. I wonder what on earth I'm going to find when we get there.

CHAPTER 25

WE TURN OFF Jamaica Street with its big parade of shops and restaurants, and travel down a warren of side roads to a well-kept low rise block of flats. Cars are parked on both sides of the road. My husband hasn't said a word since we left home, and so I try to make some conversation.

"I hope nothing comes towards us."

"It's one way."

Paul has gone into his cave, and I expect will not exit until we're back on the M8. I grab hold of his hand as he locks the car and strides across the road. There's a security phone by the entrance to the flats, and he presses the button for number 12. I hear a female voice through the intercom.

"Yes?"

"It's Paul."

There's a moment of silence before the voice speaks again.

"Oh! Well, come on up."

The main door clicks, and we step into a carpeted foyer. There's a faint aroma of cabbage, and I can hear loud music coming from one of the ground floor flats. We go upstairs to the second floor, to where a grey-haired, well-dressed woman with the same facial features as Paul who looks to be in her late forties or early fifties stands at the open door of number 12. I smile in greeting, but the woman's gaze is fixed on Paul. We go into the flat, and I follow them down a narrow hallway into the front room. The TV is blaring, and the woman turns it off before turning around to face us.

"What brings you here, son?"

"My wife wanted to meet you. Anita, this is Margaret, my mother, known as Molly. Mum, meet Anita. We were married in September."

Paul, duty done, sinks down into an armchair and stares out of the window. I hold out my hand in greeting, which is clasped in a weak handshake.

"Pleased to meet you, Anita. I never knew Paul had gone and got himself married."

I feel sorry for this seemingly normal-looking woman. I try and think of something to say."

"The wedding was a spur of the moment thing. I wanted to come here today to meet you and ask you and Paul's father if you'd both like to come to us for Christmas dinner."

At the mention of her husband, Molly's face becomes an expressionless mask.

"Paul's dad and I split up some time ago. I sold the house and moved here. It's a nice little flat, and it doesn't hold any memories."

"Oh, I'm sorry." I look at Paul, who is still staring out the window.

"Don't be." Molly smiles at me. "No, thanks for the offer, but you two have Christmas Day on your own. You don't need me hanging around like a bad smell."

I realise that I like Molly McAdam, and cannot

understand why Paul has kept her under wraps for so long. I shake my head.

"No, we'd really like you to come; honestly."

Molly looks at Paul, who is still wishing he was somewhere else, and then back at me.

"Well……"

"That's great!" Ignoring my silent husband I blabber on. "I hope you like turkey?"

"I do. Thank you ever so much, and you don't have to pick me up; I have a car. Can I get you some coffee or tea? Paul, you want some coffee?"

"Yeah."

Paul still seems morose.   I make as up-beat a reply as I can.

"Great; tea with milk and one sugar please. Thanks."

As Molly goes off into the kitchen, I take a seat next to Paul.

"Your mum's lovely! Thanks for bringing me here."

"She's okay; I could have done a lot worse." "How long has she been on her own?" "About four years."

"Why didn't you bring me here to meet her sooner?"

He shrugs and declines to give any more information. I think that for the moment it's best not to push him any further. I accept Molly's cup of tea, and try to think of something interesting to say to my new mother-in-law.

"We got married at Gretna Green. There was just the two of us plus a couple of witnesses."

Molly seems happier when she hears this, and comes to sit opposite us in a cream leather armchair.

"So your parents didn't go either?"

"That's right. When you come over at Christmas I'll

show you the photos. One of our witnesses had a camera and snapped away all day."

Molly smiles at me, hands around a plate of biscuits, and then looks at Paul.

"Paul, you've done very well for yourself. She's a lovely girl."

On hearing his mother's words, I feel Paul fidget next to me before sighing and looking up.

"I love her; she's the only one for me."

I'm surprised that he's suddenly decided to talk. He grabs a couple of biscuits but then sinks into silence again. I wait until I've finished chewing before venturing any more information.

"My parents are divorced. Dad remarried, but Mum never did."

Molly looked at me questioningly with brown eyes so like Paul's.

"Do you keep in touch with your dad?"

"Yes." I nod. Dad lives in Edinburgh. It was while I was up visiting him from London that I met Paul. Does Paul's dad visit sometimes?"

"No." Paul stood up. "Come on; it's time we were going."

Stunned at his sudden interruption, I stand but remember my manners at the last minute.

"Thanks so much for the tea, Molly. See you on Christmas Day. Have you been to Paul's flat?"

"Yes. Don't worry; I know where it is."

Paul visibly relaxes on the homeward journey. Me, I am a seething mass of questions which at that precise moment do not look as though they are ever going to be answered by my husband, who is going out of his way to give me as little information as possible. I am now so curious about Paul's father that I am determined somehow to get Molly on her own on Christmas Day to see if we can have a little girly chat over the washing up. Perhaps she might let something slip that would put me out of my misery.

CHAPTER 26

IT FEELS REALLY strange; a Christmas Day without Mum, and my first one as a married woman. I can see my present already there at the end of the bed when I'm woken up by Paul bringing in tea and toast.

"Wow! Breakfast in bed, *and* a present! Thank you!"

I sit up in bed and take the tray off him. He's grinning like a Cheshire cat who's got the cream.

"Make the most of it. Happy Christmas!"

He throws off his dressing gown, gives me a kiss, and climbs into bed beside me. I look at the large box-shaped present as we eat toast side by side companionably.

"What's in it?" I ask him in-between mouthfuls.

"That's for you to find out."

Breakfast over, I reach down inside my bedside cabinet and bring out my carefully wrapped gift for him. He looks at it in total surprise, and then back at me.

"You've bought me a present?"

"Of course!" I shrug. "It's Christmas isn't it?"

I can see his hands are shaking as he takes the parcel. He doesn't rip off the paper, but carries on staring at it. I laugh and give him a nudge.

"Aren't you going to open it then?"

"No." He shakes his head. "Not yet. I'm savouring it; it's the first Christmas present I've ever had."

I cannot believe what I've just heard, and stare at him incredulously. His eyes are swimming with tears.

"You're joking, yeah?"

"No; I'm serious." He wipes his eyes impatiently with the back of his hand. "Just leave me be a minute."

Embarrassed at showing weakness, Paul turns away. I cuddle up to his back and put my hands around his waist.

"Don't worry about being upset. *I* would be if I'd never had a present before."

Gripping the parcel like his life depended on it, Paul lowers his head and stays silent. We sit on the edge of the bed as though we're in a still-life painting, neither of us wanting to move. Eventually I pull away, not wishing to ask probing questions and upset him even further.

"I'm going to open my present now."

He nods, turns back, and watches me unwrap layers of tissue paper to reveal an expensive looking pair of black leather boots.

"I love them!" I look them over, noticing a side zip, a Cuban heel, and red fur lining.

"I've got the receipt if they don't fit."

His voice still sounds rather shaky. I put an arm across his shoulders and kiss him full on the lips.

"Thank you so much." I whisper. "I love you."

"I love you too."

He hugs me fiercely and cries like a lost soul when he opens my parcel to reveal a brand new watch. I must admit his reaction startles me, as it's something I've never seen before. We stay in bed cuddling each other until it's time for me to get up and put the turkey in the oven.

Molly arrives at four o'clock, and is embarrassed when I produce a small gift for her from under the tree.

"For me? Oh goodness!" She shakes her head. "We've never been ones for Christmas presents before. Sorry, I just didn't think to buy any."

"Don't worry about it." I hope my voice sounds reassuring enough. "Let me know next year if you'd rather not receive anything."

"It's just that there was never any money to buy presents with when the boys were small." Molly sighs. "I got out of the habit."

She seems genuinely pleased to receive a bottle of Je Reviens Eau de Toilette spray. Her face, so like Paul's, breaks into a smile, which makes her look 10 years younger. Paul even manages to join in the conversation at dinner with the help of a generous amount of Jack Daniels' lubrication. I serve up roast turkey with parsnips, roast potatoes, carrots, broccoli, peas, and pigs in blankets. After drinking three glasses of wine, two little red spots appear on Molly's cheeks, and she's as happy as a pig in the brown stuff. We pull crackers, open another bottle of wine to toast in the New Year, and I have one of those warm feelings creeping over me that you get when everything is going well.

After dinner Paul clears the table and insists on washing up to thank me for a wonderful dinner. I take the opportunity to chat to Molly in the front room, who is slightly the worse for wear.

"I'm not used to wine." Molly giggles, unusually animated. "My head is fuzzy."

"You can crash on our sofa tonight if you like." I smile at her. "We're off to see my mum tomorrow, so you can sleep in as long as you like."

"You're so kind. I can't remember when I've enjoyed a Christmas Day more."

She suddenly looks as though she might cry. I seize a chance which I reason might never occur again.

"Doesn't Paul's dad ever come to visit at Christmas?"

I bite my lip in anticipation of her reply. Molly lets out a snort of laughter.

"No, he's best where he is."

I can't help but dig a little deeper.

"And where's that then?"

Molly puts a finger to her lips and grins.

"Shhh! Never you mind, my girl. Just be thankful he's gone."

There's something about the tone of her voice that sends a shiver up my spine. Molly closes her eyes and after a few moments her head drops to her chest. I get up and go off to the kitchen to help Paul, who is swaying slightly as he scrubs pots and pans. He burps at me and grins inanely.

"Hey, beautiful girl!"

He's as pissed as a newt, but trying not to show it. I kiss his cheek and pick up a tea towel.

"Your mum's asleep. I think she's had a nice day."

"Thanks for organising it, baby."

His voice sounds slightly slurred, and I try to keep my voice even and hope for the best as I reply.

"It's a shame your dad couldn't come as well."

There's a slight hesitation before Paul bangs down a saucepan onto the draining board.

"That wanker! He got what was coming to him!"

His voice chills me to the bone, and I almost drop a plate. Paul laughs and holds onto the sink to steady himself. I suddenly don't want to hear any more. Nothing else is said, but for me Christmas Day is now definitely spoilt.

CHAPTER 27

THERE'S SOMETHING SPECIAL about being in Edinburgh on New Year's Eve. Paul and I are lucky to live just 30 minutes' walk from where the main celebrations take place, and after dinner we join huge crowds at the barriers just outside Princes Street. Paul is upbeat and looking forward to the night ahead as he waves our First Footing tickets at the bouncers.

"Hurry up!" He shouts good-naturedly. "It's my birthday! My wife's bought me a new shirt, and I wanna partaaay!"

"Shh!" I give him a nudge. "They'll blacklist us before the night's even begun!"

We move slowly along through the barriers. I'm not too keen on being in the middle of a large amount of people, and stay close to Paul. However, once we're in Princes Street the crowd disperses enough for me to look about and see what's going on.

One of the bands has already set up and is blasting out classic rock by the skating rink. Already people are dancing. High above on the hill the castle is lit with powerful brightly coloured searchlights, and down on Princes Street there are many stalls selling hot dogs, burgers, chips, and soft drinks. All around us are excited revellers shouting and singing, anxious to see in the New Year with style.

"Come on; let's hit one of the pubs for now. We can come out later on when we've had a few!"

Paul pulls me past one of the giant TV screens set up along the road, and we go into the nearest pub. A welcoming blast of warmth hits me as soon as we walk through the door, and I ask for a whisky and lemonade to keep the cold at bay. The pub is heaving. I look at my watch while I wait for Paul to come back from the bar; it's ten thirty. Another hour and a half to go until 2001. I give a rueful laugh; if somebody had told me a year ago that I would be an old married lady before the year was out, I would never have believed them.

I'm not keen on being crammed in the pub like a sardine in a tin, but as it's also Paul's birthday, I for one am not going to spoil it for him by moaning that I'd rather be outside. I suffer the noise, raucous laughter and jostling, until my husband has managed to pour three pints of beer down his neck, has had a joke with a few mates he recognises, and is now seemingly joviality personified.

"Can we see what's going on outside?" "Sure."

It's half past 11 and celebrations are in full swing. A tribute band is playing near the TV screen, and Paul grabs me for a dance. We sway in the street as Modjo's latest song starts up, kissing and cuddling like the newlyweds we still are.

"Lady, hear me tonight, 'cause my feeling is just so right!"

Paul has quite a good singing voice. I join in and press my lower body against his, enjoying the feel of his slow-growing erection as I sing.

"As we dance by the moonlight, can't you see you're my de-light!"

His arms clamp about my waist and I look up into his eyes. I suddenly want to make 2001 so right for him. I want to banish away all the hurt and anger he's had to suffer at the hands of his father, and show him just what a happy family can be like.

"Two thousand and one is going to be our year!"

"Too right, baby!"

I kiss him and enjoy the feel of his tongue winding around mine. When a slow number plays we move as one to the rhythm. I close my eyes and savour the moment.

At ten minutes to twelve we finish our hot dogs and Paul looks up towards the castle.

"Let's go up and be ready for the fireworks."

Huge numbers of people have appeared from out of nowhere, all pushing, shoving and shouting, blowing whistles, letting off party poppers, and blocking our path to the castle. I realise we will have to walk through the throng and out the other side to get to Castlehill. Paul takes my hand, knowing that I'm not comfortable in the midst of a crowd.

"Don't worry; just hold on to me and you'll be fine."

I fail to be comforted by his words; I just want to be out of the crowd. Gingerly I move into the middle of the writhing sea of humanity. Beyond the masses I can see a TV screen flickering into life, ready to beam footage of the fireworks to the assembled revellers down in Princes Street and around the globe. A voice over a loudspeaker reminds us there is only five minutes to go before the end of 2000, and a loud cheer ensues. I hang onto Paul and realise that there is no way we're going to make the castle in time for the fireworks, there are just too many people in the way.

"It's no good!" I shout to Paul in front of me. "We'll never make it!"

"Oh yes we will! We're...."

The rest of his reply is drowned out by a whistle blowing nearby. I start to feel trapped in the crowd all pushing this way and that, and begin to panic, screaming at Paul as loudly as I can.

"I want to get out! Get me out!"

I'm crying as he turns around towards me. Suddenly, as though a switch has activated in his brain, he lashes out at the drunken partygoers in front of him.

"Fuck off out the way! Move!"

To my horror he lets go of me, and begins to indiscriminately kick and punch his way forwards, ignoring counter blows raining down upon his head by angry victims. I'm screaming at him to stop, but it's like he's gone crazy in a world of his own, sweating profusely and frothing at the mouth with spittle. People are trying to move out of our way and I'm pushed to the outside of the crowd, where I collapse in a heap on the pavement, spent, frightened beyond belief at the change in my husband, and absolutely distraught. Paul exits the melee still punching and kicking, while desperately searching up and down for me as the countdown to midnight begins. There is blood dripping down his forehead, and what is even more worrying, I can also see the faintest hint of enjoyment etched on his features.

"Don't just sit there!" He pants as he catches sight of me. "You want to see the fucking fireworks don't you? Come on!"

Sobbing I run after him up Castlehill as the countdown

comes to an end. A loud rocket explodes in the sky as Big Ben's chimes sound out from another TV screen near the castle. It's 2001, I'm 18, and I'm not sure who on earth I've married.

PART 3 - PAUL
CHAPTER 28
JANUARY 3rd 2001

MARRIED LIFE IS agreeing with me, the original horse's arse of just one year ago. Darren will piss himself laughing when he hears I only had three pints on New Year's Eve. Thinking about it, perhaps it's better he *doesn't* know; I'll never live it down.

So where *is* the twat? I pick up my phone and call him once more, but all I get is the answerphone. I decide to leave a message this time.

'Dee, it's Paul. Why aren't you at work today? Still hungover? Where the fuck are you? Doddy's going apeshit. Give us a ring, mate.'

There's nothing worse than going back to work after the festive season is over. All the decorations are still up in the office, but they look kind of dejected and tacky. The only light on the horizon today will be watching Melanie's red hair falling down her back as she stands on a chair and takes them down; the decorations that is, not her knickers. Fat chance of that, but then again I don't actually care what Melanie's got under her skirt anyway; Anita gives me everything I need.

Darren's chair is still empty after the lunch break. It's a good thing nothing new has come in over the holidays. Doddy's prowling around like a bitch on heat; if I didn't need the money so much I'd slap him one and tell him to go to hell.

Anita's quiet as we drive home. I'm not sure if it's post-Christmas blues or PMT blues. It's got to be one or the other; the PMT drives me round the fucking bend. She's not long had a period so it can't be that, unless it's just my luck I've married a girl who's two weeks coming on and two weeks going off.

I risk being shot down as I speak, and look over at her as we pull up at some traffic lights.

"Alright? You're not saying much. Something I've done?"

I bite my tongue and resist adding *again* at the end of the sentence. She doesn't look at me, but carries on staring out through the front windscreen.

"I had a visit from the police today in the office."

I am instantly on the alert, and even miss the lights changing to green as I carry on watching her. When a driver honks his horn behind me I give him the finger and then pull away, still waiting for her to speak.

"What did they want?"

"That DC Elliott and somebody else came in to see me. They took away all the timesheets for April last year."

A sinking feeling shoots through my guts. Suddenly I think I know the reason why Darren's not at work.

"Did they say anything to you apart from asking for the timesheets?"

"No." Anita shakes her head. "Doddy wanted to know what it was all about, but I didn't know, as they weren't giving anything away."

Bastards! The lot of them! And there was I thinking that Darren was a mate!

After dinner I manage to convince Anita that I'm going down the Rat and Pigeon with Darren. Instead I pull up outside his bedsit and wait in the car when there's no answer to my knocking. The evening trundles by; the place remains in darkness, and my phone calls go unanswered. I sit stewing with anger, assuming he's either in bed asleep at seven o'clock in the evening, or is trying to avoid me and is staying somewhere else for the time being. I rather favour the latter.

As half ten approaches and there is still no sign of Darren, I decide to give the Rat and Pigeon a visit so that Anita will get a whiff of hops later on. Well, it would be rude not to, wouldn't it?

Ray gives me a nod when he sees me come in. I have quick scope around the place, but on a dismal night in early January the place is nearly empty. I make my way to the bar and order a beer.

"How's it going, Ray?"

Ray shakes his head and pours me a pint.

"The place is dead tonight. Haven't seen you about for a while."

"I've been playing the dutiful husband." I laugh out loud. "Has Darren been in?"

"Yeah." Ray nods at me. "But not since New Year's Eve; he was with a new girl who told me she works at Dodd's as well."

"Long ginger hair?"

"That's the one; he seemed keen on her."

Melanie. It was news to me, and I down the pint in one go.

"I'd better be off otherwise Anita will do her nut. See you soon."

"Hang loose Paul."

Anita's still sitting up watching TV when I return. I slide in next to her on the settee, and give her a kiss.

"Hi." She snuggles up closer. "Had a good evening?"

"Not bad." I lie. "Did you know Darren's going out with Melanie?"

"Is he?" Anita yawns. "No, I didn't know that."

"I wonder if he'll give up his bedsit and move in with her?"

Anita snorts.

"It's a bit soon for that isn't it? Anyway, she shares with Sue and Carol from Finance. I'm sure they wouldn't want *him* living there."

"He'll need to shower more regularly." I chuckle. "Where's their flat then?"

"Oh, over on the estate down Meadow Way I think. Why?"

"No reason." I shrug. "Just wondered. Coming to bed?"

She flicks the remote, turns off the TV, and stands up. "Okay."

Meadow Way is on the outskirts of a nearby council estate

built in the 1970's. Luckily it's a dead end, and so as I sit at the top end of the road in my car under cover of darkness I know I won't miss any comings or goings. It's eight o'clock at night, and I'm hoping Darren fancies visiting the chippy around the corner, whose welcoming yellow light I can see shining out onto the pavement.

I shiver and let the engine run for a bit to warm up the car's interior. I'm just contemplating buying some chips to keep me going, when towards nine thirty a burly figure wearing a dark hoodie and black tracksuit trousers emerges from one of the maisonettes at the other end of the road. I strain my eyes, but it's not until he passes under a streetlight that I can tell who it is. His eyes are downcast as he walks along with hunched shoulders towards the chippy. I slide down in the seat as he mooches past, and wait until he turns the corner before getting out of the car and following him, hiding out of the light down a side alley running alongside the shop.

I'm ready to pounce like one of those vultures you see hovering over a corpse in Wild West films as I catch sight of him coming out of the chippy. Sneaking out of the alley and checking the coast is clear, I place myself squarely in front of Darren just as he pops a hot chip into his mouth.

"How are you going to eat the rest of those with no fucking teeth?"

I let go a punch to his jaw. He falls back onto the pavement, dropping the chips in surprise. I stand there breathing heavily, with fists bunched ready for anything he's going to throw at me. He stumbles to his feet, holding the side of his face.

"I can explain! Let me explain!"

"So....explain then."

I push him back down the side alley, and stand over him menacingly. With one hand holding his jaw and the other lifted towards me in supplication, he leans back against the wall and gives it his best shot.

"Do you want to share the reward money? I could do with ten thousand to put a deposit down on a house; and so could you."

The bloke's got some front, I'll give him that. I knee him swiftly in the balls, and he drops down like a stone.

"How can I spend ten thousand pounds in prison, you fucking bastard! You sold me down the river! Well, it's my word against yours!" I bend down and whisper in his ear. "You'd better get another job; if you turn up at Dodd's again mate, you're dead meat."

CHAPTER 29

DC ELLIOTT IS waiting for me as Anita and I leave Dodd's and make our way to the car park. I had been expecting a visit at home, but am surprised to see him standing there.

"Hello Paul."

Out of the corner of my eye I can see Anita looking at me questioningly. Keeping my voice even I open the car door and usher Anita inside.

"Hi."

There's another cop sitting in a Ford Focus, which is blocking my exit out of the car park. DC Elliott gives me a smile that doesn't quite reach his eyes.

"Paul, we'd like you to come down to the station."

"What for?"

Anita's getting out of the car again. I wanted to spare her this, but it's not to be.

"What's going on?"

She looks at me, and I play it cool.

"They want to ask me some questions at the station, so you drive home and I'll see you later."

"What questions? What about? No, I'm coming with you!"

Other workers are starting up their engines and moving towards the car park's blocked exit. To avoid any more hassle I shrug my shoulders and follow Elliott to the Ford Focus, turning to look at Anita over my shoulder.

"Follow me down then. This won't take long."

The journey is taken in silence. I look out of the window and act as though a ride in a police car is something I do every day. Anita's driving up their exhaust pipe, and is already running ahead up the steps of the police station as we arrive. I'm determined not to give them an inch.

"Come this way."

I don't know whereabouts Anita is waiting for me, but I do know one thing; they'll get nothing out of me. I'm taken to what seems like the same interview room I was in last year. I play for time.

"I want a lawyer."

"Why? We only want to ask a couple of questions. A lawyer would mean you'd have to wait here for hours until he turns up."

I shrug and fix Elliott with a stare.

"Paul, we're following up a lead we've had regarding the murder of Catherine Taylor."

Here it comes. I keep silent and inwardly sigh.

"A fellow worker at Dodd's Computers has told me that you asked him to specifically clock you back in after lunch on the afternoon of Friday seventh April last year, the day of the murder."

"No; that's not true."

I'm loving it.

"He confirms that he clocked you back in at twelve

thirty, but that you did not actually re-appear until two o'clock. Is that correct?"

"No; why would he say that? I always have half an hour for lunch, and it's fish and chips on Fridays. I'm always back at work by half past twelve every day."

"Where were you on the afternoon of Friday seventh April last year between the hours of twelve noon and two o'clock?"

"Half an hour for fish and chips, and then back at work; I've just told you. Have a look at my timesheet."

"We did."

"And?"

"And it says you took half an hour for lunch."

"Well, there you go then; that's what I did."

"But Mr Maynard says you asked him to clock you in because you'd told him you would not be back until two o'clock, and that you would be down on hours if he didn't, as you had not gained enough time in credit to take a two hour lunch break."

"He's lying; he's only said that to get the reward. It's amazing what people will do and say when a large amount of money's at stake."

They've got nothing on me, and they know it. If they think a visit to the police station is going to unnerve me, then they've got another think coming.

Anita is waiting for me in Reception, unsmiling and looking anxious. I give her the thumbs up, but she still looks serious. With one arm around her shoulders I saunter out of the cop shop with as much swagger as I can muster.

I can't put my finger on it, but there's something wrong with

Anita. For the past week since my police interview she's been quiet and reserved. I've tried to jolly her along, but she's not going for it. She's even distant in bed, which is not like her at all.

After a silent journey home from work today and an evening meal where she's hardly spoken more than two words to me, I'm starting to get the willies big time. I help her to wash up after dinner, and even hoover around the flat wearing just a smile, one of her bras padded out with socks, and a pinny fashioned out of a tea towel. There's a faint upturn of one corner of her mouth as I pout and preen around the front room like Freddie Mercury gone wrong, and wiggle my bum. Her response is encouraging, although slightly disappointing at the same time.

"Hey!" I carefully suck up a corner of the tea towel with the hoover pipe. "Wanna see what's under my pinny?"

She cannot help herself, and gives out a throaty chuckle.

"No! Put it away!"

"Aw….he wants to say hello; he hasn't seen you all week!"

She sinks onto the sofa and switches on the TV. I feel a total prat standing there in a bra and tea towel, but I know that if she asked me to I'd parade along the pavement outside wearing them if it would make things right between us again.

I put the vacuum cleaner away, get dressed into something more suitable, and sit myself down next to her on the settee. Immediately I feel her freezing up, and so refrain from putting my arms around her.

"What's wrong, hinny? What have I done?"

I'm at a loss for what to do to please her. Suddenly I think of something all girls want.

"Hey, how about stopping your pill and we try for a baby?"

She looks at me as if I've grown three heads.

"Paul, I'm eighteen years old for God's sake! Let me live a bit first, eh?"

She turns back to the TV and I have cold chills down my back and a scary thought that I might be losing her. I tread on eggshells and try one more time.

"Please. What's the matter?"

She turns off the television and faces me.

"I went to the library last Saturday when I was out shopping, and got them to look up your dad's name on the old microfiche newspapers."

I try and stop my hands bunching up, as my heart starts racing away like I've just run up Castlehill.

"Why did you do that?"

"Because I want to know what's happened to him. I read an article that said his brother reported him missing three years ago."

She sounds at the end of her rope. I move closer and risk a bollocking.

"He's not missing. He just went off with some other woman, that's all; broke Mum's heart. Good riddance to the fucker, that's what I say."

The years of drunken beatings, bruises, Mum's tears, and Terry's move to Australia rush to the forefront of my mind. I see my father standing over me with a baseball bat. It was the last thing he ever did.

"It said his bank account hadn't been used."

"I don't know anything about that. He had a joint account with Mum; that's all I know."

She doesn't look convinced. Her next question floors me completely.

"Paul…did you have anything to do with your father's disappearance?"

"What a bloody question!" I stand up and begin pacing about the room. "I just told you he went off with somebody else! So now you think I've bumped him off?"

She puts her head in her hands.

"I don't know what to think anymore. You seem so…...*angry* sometimes!"

She begins to sob in that heart-breaking way that only women can. I want to wrap her up in my arms and never let her go. She's my rock and my future; the only person who can keep me from the gates of hell.

"Please don't cry." I run over to her, kneel down, and put both arms around her waist. "Dad wanted nothing more to do with us. If he ever turns up again you'll see what a complete waster he is."

"I so want to believe you, Paul. I really do."

She looks straight through me, but I see a chink appearing in her armour.

"Then believe me. Forget about my father. We've got a good life ahead of us."

She smiles at me and I kiss her, relieved beyond words.

CHAPTER 30

I KEEP A close eye on Anita, but she still doesn't seem like her old self. She walks about like all the stuffing's been knocked out of her. About a week later we're sitting down to dinner and she gives out one of those thin little smiles that really puts the wind up me.

"What?" I stop chewing for a moment and look at her.

"DC Elliott brought the timesheets back today." "So?"

"So, he was asking me about you; about your personality."

I put down my knife and fork for a moment.

"And you told him I've got about as much charm as a dead slug?"

"No, of course not." She grimaces again. "I told him you're alright, but just on a bit of a short fuse sometimes, that's all."

"Why did you go and say something like that?" I glare at her. "You're supposed to be on my side!"

"I *am* on your side, Paul, but I think you have anger management problems. Your temper frightens me. When you get angry it's like you're another person, somebody I don't want to be with."

She's looking down into her plate, and I'm terrified. I'm having trouble managing a rising feeling of annoyance at the thought of Elliott trying to spoil what Anita and I have together.

"Why are you even talking to that fucker?" I stand up and look down on her. "It's obvious he's trying to blame somebody for Cat's murder to win himself a medal, and I'm a prime target!"

"How could I ignore him when he was standing there asking me questions? I don't want any more dinner; I'm not hungry."

She puts down her knife and fork and pushes her chair back. As it scrapes across the lino I get a flashback of Dad doing the self-same thing before flinging his plate of food at my head to stop me tapping my fingers on the table. I see Mum standing up trying to protect me, but receiving a punch in the eye for her trouble.

"Finish your dinner!" I'm shouting now to block out the memories. "We're going to sit here like every other normal couple does and eat our food together. It's what married people do!"

"Fuck off!" Anita stands up and starts running away. "I don't want to eat with you!"

A red rage takes me over, and I upend the table. Plates still holding the remnants of our meal smash to the floor, along with drinking glasses and half a bottle of burgundy, which spills out over the lino like a trickling river of blood.

"Get back in here!"

I rush after her, but am too late as Anita screams, runs to the bedroom, and locks herself in. The anger is all –

consuming now. I put my shoulder to the door and then give it a kick. The door gives way easily and I see my wife cowering in a corner, holding up a chair in front of her. She is sobbing, with eyes like those of a hunted fox set upon by a pack of hounds.

"Leave me alone or I'll call the police!"

I see my mother curling up into a ball to protect herself from the blows raining down upon her, and I realise I'm turning into my bastard of a father. In a trice the anger subsides, and all I want to do is run over to Anita and hold her tight. I back off into the hallway.

"I'm sorry!" I shake my head and continue retreating. "I'm sorry!"

We stand there for what seems like an eternity looking at each other, each wondering what the other is going to do next. Finally Anita puts the chair down and sinks to the floor, weeping silently.

"You're a pig of a man; an absolute pig!"

I change my mind and begin to inch nearer to her, keeping my hands by my sides.

"Stay away from me!"

She looks startled as I edge towards her.

"I'm not going to hurt you; I love you, for God's sake!" I sit down on the end of the bed, sigh, and hold up the palms of my hands.

"What happens now?"

Anita edges past me, making for the door which is now hanging off its hinges.

"What happens now is that I move out, which is something I should have done a long time ago. In fact, thinking about it, I don't know how I could have been so stupid as to marry you in the first place!"

The plan for our happy-ever-after future is unravelling at an alarming rate. I cannot, *will* not let my wife go.

"This will never happen again, d'you hear me?" I stand up, distraught. "I'll seek help; I know I've got a problem. Help me, don't leave me! Please!"

She stops in her tracks.

"Did you kill your father, Paul?"

I sigh and shake my head.

"No, I didn't."

"What happened to him then?"

I can still see the bastard in my mind towering over me, telling me I was no son of his. I sink down to my knees and put my head in my hands, wiping away tears and wanting to push the long-buried memory away.

"He was about to finish me off with a baseball bat. Terry got hold of a carving knife just in time, and stuck it between his ribs. If he hadn't done it, Mum would have. The fucker's dead and buried. It's why Terry went to Australia; he started a new life, and good luck to him. I should have done the same."

It's like a bolt of lightning has shot through Anita. She comes over to me, kneels down, and I put my head in her lap. Years of beatings, torture and heartache escape from me in one huge sob, as she strokes my hair.

"Where is your dad buried?"

I wait until I can stop crying long enough to answer her without sounding like I'm drunk or that I've got a speech defect.

"I'm not even sure he is my dad; he told me enough times that he wasn't. It's not the sort of thing you can ask your mother though, is it?" I pause for breath. "With Mum's blessing I helped Terry to bury Dad and the knife ten feet under a concrete patio that Terry laid at my parents' old house. If the new owners ever decide to dig it up, then they'll get a bit of a shock. He'd been under there a year before his brother even realised he was gone; thank God they weren't close. The police interviewed Mum; but of course she wasn't giving anything away. She told them he wasn't missing and that he'd just buggered off with somebody else."

The relief of telling somebody is overwhelming. I didn't ever envisage laying all our family's dirty laundry at my wife's feet, but in a way I'm glad the secret is out in the open. I feel like a huge weight has been lifted from my shoulders, but of course this will not go anywhere in helping me with the immediate problem of Anita threatening to leave me.

I lift my head from her lap and stare at the face I want to look at for the rest of my life.

"I couldn't bear it if you go; please give me another chance."

She takes a huge breath and sighs.

"What about Catherine Taylor?"

"What about her?" I shrug. "Were

you involved in her death?"

"No, of course not!" I shake my head. "One of her clients obviously got a little too rough."

"Why did Darren cover for you then, on the day of her murder like the police are saying?"

I get slowly to my feet and sink onto the bed.

"He didn't. He was after the reward money and made up a story."

"Why hasn't he come back to work?"

"He found another job."

She comes and sits beside me. I put my arms around her and bury my face in her hair.

"Forgive me; I'm the biggest arsehole who ever lived."

"No you're not." Anita kisses me. "You're my husband and I love you."

I squeeze her tightly and we sit there together like statues for some time, until reluctantly I pull away and go off to make some semblance of order out of the shattered glass and encrusted spaghetti Bolognese splattered all over the kitchen.

CHAPTER 31

ANITA'S FOUND SOME anger management classes run by some twat in a suit called Nigel. Nigel is peculiarly serene, and looks as though he's never shouted at anybody in his whole life. Just why Nigel wants to spend two evenings a week with a group of sad fuckers like us is anyone's guess.

There's Joe, who has Tourette's syndrome and yells at everyone and anyone for the sheer joy of it. There's Kayleigh, who's a chain smoker outside of the classroom and a dab hand at putting cigarette burns on the skin of anyone who pisses her off, and there's Ryan, who is a little pressure cooker waiting to explode all by himself and so far hasn't said a bloody word. My favourite though is Michael, who's just got out of prison early for manslaughter after bludgeoning his wife to death when he found her with another man, and has to take the classes as part of his rehabilitation. Anita is thrilled that I'm even attending in the first place, and I'm loving it; mixing with the kind of people my mother always warned me about.

Tonight Nigel has a cold, and is constantly sniffing. It's pissing us all off, and sooner or later there's going to be a riot. However, before we all jump up and throttle him, Nigel wants us to discuss some test questions to determine how angry we still are after managing to sit through six of his classes. Me, I don't feel any different, but it's keeping Anita happy.

Nigel's adenoidal tones drift over my head as I wonder whether Anita's ready for sex yet. So far since the Spag-Bol-all-over-the-kitchen episode she's only let me cuddle her in bed, but truth be told I'm surprised she's even let me do that.

"……..*and despite its reputation, anger is not a bad emotion in and of itself. It's our individual reaction to anger that determines how helpful or harmful it can be.*"

I yawn as Nigel prattles on, with nobody listening.

"….*and with a better understanding of anger and how to deal with it, we can learn to identify our own personal style of coping and work on developing a more positive and productive approach.*"

I must admit, our coping strategies suck big time. I pick up the multiple choice test paper and glance at the questions. I want to laugh out loud at the first one:

'*On your way home from work you stop at the supermarket and see your partner kissing somebody very passionately in the fruits and vegetables section. Until this moment you thought your relationship was stable and loving. How angry does this make you feel?*'

I mean, who wouldn't feel angry and want to kick the bloke in the fruits and vegetables? I put up my hand and Nigel gives me a smile.

"Yes, Paul. Do you wish to start off the discussion?" "I'd feel very angry about number one, Nigel, furious in fact. Wouldn't you? Wouldn't anyone?"

"Of course! But it's how you deal with that anger; that's the point I'm trying to get over."

"So instead of kicking the bloke into the bread and cakes section, you sit down with your partner and discuss why you're such a shithole that it's caused her to do the dirty on you and look elsewhere?"

Nigel beams at me through a tissue.

"Paul, you're learning more every time you come here! But also, if you remember from last week, you mustn't take everything personally and believe that a partner would stray because it's something you yourself did. People have their own reasons for doing something. When you are immune to opinions, behaviours and actions of others, then you will not be a victim of needless suffering any longer."

I sigh and take one of Nigel's deep, calming breaths, counting to 11 as I breathe out.

"But I've got to take it personally if I see my partner necking in Sainsbury's with another bloke?"

"Yeah, I'd take it personally alright!" Michael the manslaughterer nods in agreement.

"I'd nut him one." Kayleigh adds. "What about you, Ryan?"

Silence.

"Discussion always works better, Kayleigh, if you remember from past classes." Nigel sneezed. "Find out why your partner has strayed. It may be because they feel unloved; perhaps you've been too busy at work to show them any attention?"

"I'm on the dole."

"Work on making your relationship a positive thing. Vent your fears to your partner, but in a non-aggressive manner. Keep a journal so as not to internalise your anger; remember your calming strategies."

I can see that Joe is twitching, ready to explode.

"You're all fucking wankers!"

I hide a grin behind my test paper.   Nigel's visage

remains serene as he visualises idyllic scenes of lambs frolicking in flower-bedecked meadows.

"Remember your calming aids, Joe." "Up yours!"

When I get home Anita's watching TV. She looks up from her programme as I come into the front room.

"How'd it go?"

"Peachy. I mustn't take anything personally, even if I catch you snogging in Sainsbury's with Darren."

She laughs, and it's a wonderful tinkling sound that I haven't heard in a long time.

"Why would I want to snog Darren in Sainsbury's?"

"To get at his fruits and vegetables."

"Give over!" She snorts. "*I'd* take it extremely personally though, if I caught you snogging Melanie under the mistletoe."

"But you wouldn't want to kill me?" She shakes her head.

"I might *say* it, but no, I wouldn't *do* it."

"I've got to learn calming strategies. Apparently if I count to eleven, write my feelings down in a diary, go for a walk, relax in a bath, or listen to music, then I won't feel like mutilating anybody."

"Sounds good to me; especially if it's me that's going to be mutilated for snogging in Sainsbury's."

We're back with the banter that's been missing from our marriage for a long time. I'm so lucky that Anita's given me a second chance, I'd try and fly to the moon if she wanted me to. I flop down on the settee and put my arms around her.

"Thanks for sticking with me. I'll make us right again."

"I know you will."

I lift her chin up and kiss her full on the lips. From her response I deduce I have a good chance of taking part in another calming strategy which Nigel hasn't mentioned thus far. I let one hand stray down to her breast, and am pleased beyond belief as she arches her back. I know without a shadow of a doubt that getting one's leg over is going to be the most calming and agreeable of all the strategies I know.

It feels so good to feel her naked body under mine. The settee squeaks in protest as we crash through pounding waves of lust, eventually riding out all our frustrations and ending up floating entwined on waters as calm and serene as the proverbial millpond.

The central heating's gone off and we're freezing when we wake up at midnight, naked and still cuddling together on the settee. I wriggle off and kiss the top of Anita's head.

"Come on; let's go to bed."

She yawns, stands up, and follows me down to the bedroom. As we climb into bed she tosses one of those remarks to me that guarantees I'll be awake for the rest of the night.

"Why don't you try and get in touch with your brother?"

I look over at her in surprise.

"I don't know where he lives, and I haven't got his phone number."

She shrugs her shoulders.

"But there's Facebook!"

"But I don't have an account."

She rolls her eyes as a mother might do whilst trying to cajole a recalcitrant teenager.

"Get one then!"

Terry. The big brother I looked up to. Anita will never know just how much I miss him.

CHAPTER 32

"ARE YOU EXPLODERS or imploders?"

Nigel looks at us, waiting for a reaction. When we all look at him blankly, he carries on.

"Take a for instance. You're in the cinema and a guy behind you starts kicking the back of your seat. You ask him to stop, but he still does it. What would you have done in the past?"

Michael the manslaughterer chips in with his opinion almost straight away.

"Nut him one."

Nigel nods sagely.

"But you all know better than that now, don't you? Instead of exploding and causing him grievous bodily harm, or sitting there *im*ploding; seething and letting your resentment build up to another inevitable *ex*plosion, what's the best thing to do based on what you've learned here? Ryan?"

Silence.

Paul?

I've been getting good at telling Nigel what he wants to hear. I've got the measure of him now. I pretend to think for a bit, and then give him the answer he wants.

"I'd move to another seat."

"Exactly! Well done Paul!" Nigel beams at me like I've just won the Nobel Peace Prize. "We use the strategy of removing ourselves physically from the situation."

I can see Kayleigh fixing me with a stare and trying to butt in.

"What happens if there's somebody else kicking the back of your seat *after* you've moved?"

"Then you spend all night traipsing round the cinema, miss the film and waste your money. You have to end up renting it on DVD so that you can sit at home like Billy-no-mates and watch it in peace."

"Prat."

I stare her out and she looks away.

I keep thinking about Terry, and the Facebook thing starts playing on my mind more and more. He was the big brother I could count on and who was always there for me; the brother who saved my life in the nick of time, and who finally gave Mum peace of mind. I know he will never return to Scotland again, but I have a sudden longing for his deep, booming laugh, and to hear him tell me that everything's going to be okay.

One evening I log on to Facebook on my laptop and open up an account while Anita's watching one of those miserable soap operas where everyone looks as though they've been hit round the face several times with a shovel.

I ask to be Anita's friend, whose page is locked to private, fill in some details about myself, and then look up Terence Ian McAdam but have no luck. However, when I search for Terry McAdam I can see my brother as large as life. He's lost a bit of hair over the past few years, but there he is sunburnt and sitting on a beach with a dark-haired woman and a little boy. I look closer at the extended family which Mum and I have been denied; Terry had obviously not taken up the advice he'd given me on the night when aged fifteen I'd announced to him that I was taking a girl out for the first time. I chuckle to myself, still hearing the *fuck 'em and forget 'em* motto which I'd strictly adhered to until I'd met Anita. The woman is good-looking in a dark, sultry kind of way, but the little boy has Terry's colouring and facial features.

Terry's page is open in a way that Anita's is not. I see that he's now 28, married to Shannon McAdam nee Drury, and that he lives in Sydney. There are quite a few photo albums to look at; the latest one is entitled *Ben's Third Birthday*. Terry's handing out sweets, swinging kids around and around, and cooking burgers on a barbeque; just a regular Aussie guy. He's popular, with 214 friends, none of which I recognise.

It occurs to me as I look through more photos that just maybe he wanted me to find him. We share a secret that binds us together despite living on opposite sides of the globe. As I look at him sunbathing on Bondi beach I idly wonder if he ever thinks of his little brother, his mum, and the life he left behind.

I send Terry a friend request, and hope for the best. There's a private message button and I can't resist that one either.

'Hi Tel, yeah I finally got on Facebook. Put another prawn on the barbie for me.'

I'm grinning to myself as I go back to the search box at the top of the page. I cannot help myself and type in

Catherine Taylor to see what comes up. I recognise her at once from all the others. The page is public, and is being run by her mother. I see photos of Cat as a little kid, all pigtails and gap-tooth grins. Then comes the Cat I kind of recognise, although she has darker hair. The £20,000 reward still stands, and my blood runs cold. There's a phone number and email address for people to get in touch with any information. Several people have already left encouraging comments that the police will eventually find the killer, but luckily none of them go by the name of Darren Maynard.

Up comes a little red 'friend accepted' notification. Anita, as usual, is sitting watching TV and checking her phone at the same time. I don't know how women do that; I can only concentrate on the television or read phone messages, but not both at the same time.

I search for Darren, but he either doesn't have a Facebook account, or has deleted it. I send a few more friend requests, and then log out when I hear strains of the soap opera's dismal tune filtering through into the bedroom.

"Hi." Anita pops her head around the door. "So you did it then!"

"Yeah." I nod. "At least I've got one friend now." "Poor bugger." She trills. "I'm sure Terry will be in touch sooner or later."

"I don't know." I shrug. "I'm sure he doesn't want to be reminded of the past; he's better off where he is."

"Blood is thicker than water; just you wait and see."

It's a week later and I've just about given up on Terry ever getting in touch. I don't blame him really; I wouldn't want to contact *me* either. I log onto Facebook just before I leave for another session with Nigel, and there's a lovely red notification to say that Terry McAdam has accepted my friend request. He's even replied to my message.

'Bloody hell, you've got married? Put some photos up.'

I feel like pogoing around the room, but I haven't got a pogo stick. Instead I rush out to the kitchen, lift Anita up, and swing her around the room. She laughs and throws her arms around my neck.

"Hey! What's going on?"

"Terry's got in touch!" I kiss her. "He said *yes!*"

"I told you he would!" She returns my kiss. "He's probably missing his little brother."

I'm the happiest one out of all of them at Nigel's class that evening. I decide that at long last I've got nothing to be angry about. My awesome wife has given me a second chance at building the happy family I've always wanted, and my long-lost brother doesn't seem to think that I'm some sad fucker to be ignored after all. There's only one black cloud on the horizon; and it's a biggie. I've a nasty feeling that Catherine Taylor is going to haunt me for the rest of my days here on earth, and while she's thinking about it will probably also balls up my chances in the afterlife as well.

CHAPTER 33

TERRY WANTS US to fly out to Sydney. He says they have a spare room and the holiday won't cost us anything other than the price of the flights. I tell him I'm all for it and will start saving for the air fare straight away, but the only problem is that Anita's not keen on the heat and the flies. He advises us to come out in July or August when it's cooler. I'm ecstatic when Anita agrees, and suddenly in just a few months I'm going to see the brother I haven't met in nearly five years.

I give up Nigel's classes; after all, I've got nothing to be angry about anymore. I'm the luckiest bastard who ever lived. Doddy hums and hars at the thought of Anita and I being out of the office for nearly three weeks in the summer, but relents eventually when I lay it on thick about not having seen Terry since I was a kid. He advises us to start saving, and I volunteer for any overtime going and keep my nose close to the grindstone. At the beginning of May we've got enough money in the bank to book the flights, but Anita has one question as we drive home from work.

"Are you going to tell your mum that we're flying out to see Terry?"

I shake my head.

"No, it's best to leave things as they are and just meet up at Christmas and birthdays. I don't think she wants us around; it reminds her too much of what happened."

"Will he want me out there? Won't he just want to see *you?*"

I look at her in surprise.

"No, of course not! He has a wife, Shannon. I'm sure the two of you will get along just fine."

Anita's buying up so many new clothes that I'm sure I'm going to have to jump on her case to close it, and it's going to cost me a fortune in extra baggage at the check in. She's starting to parade in front of me night after night like a model on the catwalk, showing off her purchases. However, all I want to do is rip the buggers off. Sometimes I've been very successful in that endeavour, but I know to only remove them very carefully so as not to risk a bollocking. That suits me fine; the slower I can take them off and feast my eyes on her body, the better I like it.

It's one of those overcast, cool mornings that passes for British summertime when the alarm wakes us up at 5am on Friday July 27th. I've only managed to sleep for a couple of hours, wondering what the hell I'm going to say to Terry after all this time. I yawn and give Anita a nudge.

"Wakey wakey! Seven hours to Abu Dhabi and then another fourteen hours overnight to Sydney coming up."

"Shit." Anita sits up and rubs her eyes. "I'm going to look like nothing on earth when I get off that plane."

I kiss her and climb out of bed.

"You'd look beautiful in a sack."

"Well, cheers for that; perhaps I shouldn't have wasted

money on all these clothes then."

"Yeah, it would have been cheaper to buy a roll of bin liners."

After breakfast it's time to leave for the airport but her bloody case won't close. I end up having to cram in a load of frilly women's stuff in my own suitcase, leaving out a couple of pairs of my jeans and some tee shirts. I'm none too pleased about it, but it would have been World War Three if I'd refused. I'm listening to Nigel's voice in my ear as I snap the cases shut whilst all the time visualising sitting in Terry's garden with a cold beer.

It's only about seven miles to Edinburgh airport, and we're there by 05:50. As the cases get shunted off down a conveyor belt at the check-in, I say a silent prayer of hope that we'll be reunited with them 10,000 miles later. Anita suggests buying presents for Terry, Shannon and Ben for putting us up for three weeks, and so I walk dejectedly around the Duty Free shops with her in the departure lounge trying to part with the least amount of money as possible. I remember that Terry smokes like a chimney, and so buy 200 cigarettes for him, some perfume for Shannon, and a cuddly toy for the nephew I've never seen.

At Abu Dhabi there's a 2 hour layoff for re-fuelling. As we step out of the plane onto the tarmac, the digital thermometer on the side of one of the airport buildings hits 36 degrees Centigrade. I exhale and walk quicker towards what I hope is the terminal's air-conditioned coolness.

"Betty's come along for the ride."

"Who?" Anita, puzzled, looks at me.

"Betty Swallocks." I grin whilst wishing I was wearing cut-off jeans instead.

Anita makes a face.

"Ugh, too much information."

As far as I can see from the local fare on offer, Arabs seem to eat a lot of humus. Anita's been trying for ages to get me to eat it, but to me it looks like the contents of a baby's nappy. I'm more your steak and chips man, and luckily for me the usual junk food outlets are inside the airport terminal. By the time we're on our way again I'm stuffed full of saturated fat and ready for a good night's kip.

Have you ever tried sleeping on an overnight flight though? When the trolley dollies eventually stop walking up and down and turn off the lights, then the snorer from hell starts up behind me and fifteen thousand toddlers out of their usual routine start giving it some welly. Anita's moaning that she's cold, and so I take off my jacket and drape it over her. The bloke in front of me lowers the back of his seat so I've got the top of his head in my face, and without my jacket *I'm* now freezing my nuts off and there's still another 12 hours to go. Still, at least Anita's warm, and once she's asleep she stops complaining.

I'm feeling something akin to the proverbial equine's rectum as we touch down at Sydney airport. Anita wakes up refreshed and raring to go, as does the bloke in front, who fortunately hasn't got a clue that I've murdered him a dozen times over during the night in my head while all the time gazing innocently out of the window. Nigel would be proud of me.

Looking round Arrivals I recognise him straight away; Terry, my wild brother, is waving frantically at me. I notice he's looking more like Dad as he gets older. He seems to be on his own, and I can see he's put on a bit of weight as I drop the cases, grin, and walk towards him. The past four and a half years drop away and I find myself enveloped in the biggest bear hug I've ever had.

"Good to see you, little brother!"

He's wearing crisp, fresh clothes, and there's an aroma of shower gel. I daren't even guess what I smell like.

"Let me go, you twat!"

He holds me at arm's length and ruffles my hair.

"Come on; Shannon's got some bacon rolls on the go." He looks around. "Where's your wife?"

"Over there." I point to Anita, all long blonde hair and fake tan, guarding the cases and smiling self-consciously.

Terry whistles softly.

"Christ; she's a looker! How come she ended up with you?"

"It's my innate charm that bowled her over."

He strides over to Anita straight away. She looks as though she's just stepped out of the pages of a fashion magazine, and as she greets him I realise I've never been more proud her than I am at this moment.

Terry keeps up a running commentary as we leave the airport and head out on the M5 South-Western motorway towards a suburb of Sydney I'm surprised to hear is called Liverpool. From what he tells us I find out that he certainly seems to have settled down, working hard as an electrician and putting a deposit down on a three bedroomed apartment close to Bigge Park so that little Ben can have somewhere to run, as I learn the apartment has a back yard just about big enough for the traditional Aussie barbeque.

Terry negotiates the traffic and I look across at Anita, whose head is swivelling from side to side taking it all in.

"Alright?"

"Sure." She beams at me. "I can't believe I'm actually here."

Terry pipes up from the front.

"When did you two get married?"

"Last September." Anita smiles at his reflection in the rear view mirror.

"Yeah" I add. "One of those Gretna Green jobbies."

Terry chuckles softly.

"Really? Did Mum go?"

"Yes really, and no she didn't." I change the subject. "How about you and Shannon?"

"We got married three years ago. Shannon was pregnant, and at last I can say I did something right."

There comes over us one of those silences which speaks volumes. Sitting behind Terry I look at the back of his head, once so familiar that as a kid I could always pick him out in a crowd. Now his hair is thinning and there's even a few grey streaks, but he's still my wild brother even though he's somewhat tamer than I remember. As he sweeps the car down a pleasant tree-lined street and pulls up on his driveway I ruminate on the fact that perhaps tame can be just as good in the long run.

There's a waft of frying bacon as we enter the apartment. A mini tornado clad in stripy pyjamas hurls itself at Terry.

"Daddy!"

I grin at my brother as he picks his son up and kisses him.

"Ben, meet your Uncle Paul and Auntie Anita."

I smile at my nephew, who looks at me shyly from the safety of his father's arms.

"Hello."

I'm not usually too good with children and don't really

know what else to say. However, Anita steps in and waves the cuddly bear in front of the boy that we bought at Edinburgh airport.

"Hi Ben, this is for you."

Ben reaches out and grabs the toy from Anita, and within minutes they're firm friends. Shannon appears from the kitchen and greets us effusively. I notice dark wavy hair, olive skin, and a face and figure something like Victoria Beckham's. I realise my brother has done very well for himself in his new life, and I suddenly think of my old mum sitting alone in her flat never knowing or recognising her little grandson or new daughter-in-law even if she happened to ever pass them in the street.

"Bacon rolls in the kitchen; come this way."

We follow Shannon down a spacious hallway into a modern fitted kitchen, off of which is an alcove holding a dining table and six chairs. I'm more tired than I've ever felt in my life and after breakfast yawn continually, suffering the effects of two days without sleep and a carbo-loaded stomach full of bacon rolls. Even a strong coffee cannot seem to work its magic. Terry wants to show us around the apartment, but truth be told all I'm looking forward to is a shower and 8 hours' sleep. Shannon comes to my rescue, points out our room with its en-suite shower facilities, and tells us to emerge when we're feeling more human. I sink down on a rather comfortable double bed and let Anita go in first for a wash.

CHAPTER 34

ANITA'S GONE WHEN I wake up in unfamiliar surroundings. I look at the bedside clock which shows 2:45. For a moment I have no idea if it's quarter to three in the morning or in the afternoon, but when I hear Ben's voice out in the yard I realise that I've slept a good part of the day away.

Feeling annoyed with myself but wonderfully refreshed, I have a quick shower and change of clothes, and then emerge out of the bedroom to find the others. The apartment is all on one level, but it seems more spacious than the flats at home. I have a quick glance about, noticing two other bedrooms leading off the central hallway, a lounge, a study, a cloakroom, a main bathroom, and the kitchen with its small dining room and door leading out into the yard. All the walls are decorated in pastel shades, and the apartment is tastefully furnished in pine, with some kind of wall-to-wall hardwearing hessian-type carpet.

I hang my head in mock embarrassment as I join the others. The temperature seems as pleasantly warm as a Scottish summer day, even though it's winter. Terry's fired up the barbeque, and Anita and Shannon are running around after Ben, who is pedalling a go-kart across the yard.

"Sorry!" I grin at our hosts. "You should have woken me up."

"Not at all." Shannon shakes her head. "Travelling takes it out of you."

Terry waves a spatula at me.

"You missed lunch, but I've got some steaks cooking for dinner. I remember what you like."

Anita's made herself at home and is pushing Ben around in his go-kart. The bacon went down hours ago and I'm starving.

"Can I do anything to help?"

I feel like I should be earning my keep. Shannon nods and indicates towards the kitchen.

"There's some bread and bowls of salad and rice on the breakfast bar. You can bring them out if you like."

I take a moment to look around the kitchen as I pile the food on a tray. Terry has added some nice spotlights in the ceiling which highlight the breakfast bar, the cooker, fridge, and the washing machine. All four walls are plastered with Ben's paintings, and the whole room has a homely feel. Shannon comes in just as I pick up the tray.

"I'll just get some beers from the fridge." I like her accent.

"You've certainly changed my brother." I smile at her. "He's a different man."

"Ah, he's grown up; Ben's seen to that." Shannon chuckles. "He's been really excited at the thought of meeting up with you again."

"Same here." I admit. "We used to be quite close."

Shannon shrugs her shoulders and looks seemingly into my soul before speaking, searching I think for that one elusive explanation I'm not prepared to give.

"I don't know why Terry came over here, but all I can say is I'm very glad he did."

"He's an Aussie through and through now; don't you worry about that."

I have a sneaky suspicion she knows I hold the exact answer to her question. All of a sudden I can't wait to get back out with the others.

At bedtime Anita's yawning but I'm raring to go, having slept most of the day away. I just about manage a cuddle before she falls asleep. I pull a jacket on over my jeans and sweatshirt, and wander out into the yard. Within ten minutes I hear the patio door sliding back, and Terry's bass tones behind me.

"I thought I heard you walking about."

"Sorry; I'm wide awake now." I grin at Terry. "This jet lag sucks doesn't it?"

"You'll be okay after a couple of days." Terry nods. "It got me at first too"

I look approvingly at my brother.

"It's a nice life you've got for yourself here."

"Yeah; there's enough work, although I've taken a fortnight off at the moment. Shannon wants another baby, so I'm doing my bit to further the McAdam dynasty as well."

"It's a tough job." I laugh. "But someone's got to do it."

"It'll be every fucking night next week when she's in the middle of her cycle."

"Bloody hell; what a nightmare." I roll my eyes to the heavens and then give him a wink. "Good luck with that then."

We seem to have already slipped into that easy relationship we had way back when. Terry slopes off to the kitchen to find a couple of beers, and we sit out in the dark enjoying the kind of camaraderie that only brothers cemented by a shared past can comprehend. Eventually I look at my watch and find the hands have moved towards one o'clock.

"Shannon will be wondering where you are." I stand up, a little unsteadily after helping Terry put half a bottle of whisky to bed. "It's time we called it a night."

"Tell Anita that Shannon's taking her down to the McQuarie Street shopping mall tomorrow… er today." Terry slurred. "We can take Ben over to the park and run him around with a ball."

"Sounds great." I yawn. "See you later."

I make my way down the hallway, and Anita is warm and soft when I cuddle up to her back. In no time I'm in the land of nod again.

The good thing about being an uncle is that you can kick a football around with your little nephew, but then hand him back to his parents at the end of the day. I'm all for having babies in the future, but Anita's right, she's just a kid herself, and I'm not ready for fatherhood and the sight of someone else's face in my wife's titties where mine should be.

Ben's a good kid though, who seems to have taken a bit of a shine to me. I let him score an easy goal past me and grin at Terry.

"It's a pity they can't be born at three years old isn't it?"

"Oh, I don't know." Terry smiles at his son. "It's different when it's your own baby. You can put up with the shit and the sleepless nights."

"You're not selling it very well."

Terry gives out one of those big, booming laughs that I remember so well, and claps me on the back.

"Give it time, little brother. You can't stop the women wanting kids; it's inbuilt in them. Wait until Anita hits thirty, and then it'll get worse. Shannon's nearly there, already worrying about her biological clock ticking away."

"I can't ever imagine being a father, but if I ever do have a kid I know one thing." I look round at Terry. "I'll be doing a better job of it than Dad did."

Terry kicks the ball to Ben, who giggles and runs after it.

"It was the drink that ballsed it all up for him. If I'm looking after Ben and Shannon's out, I never touch a drop." I look at Ben, happy and smiling, and remember the arguments, the shouting and the beatings.

"We had a crap time of it, didn't we?"

Terry makes no comment straight away, because really, there's nothing left *to* say. However, I'm unprepared for the conspiratorial wink that comes just before my brother gives me a huge grin.

"Never mind; I made it all better didn't I?"

The girls are getting on like a house on fire, chatting away as though they've known each other all their lives. On the third night we go into town for an early meal so that Ben doesn't get too tired. Apparently, according to Terry, toddlers have a tendency to throw food around or fall flat into their dinner if they haven't had an afternoon nap. There's a nice restaurant down Memorial Avenue that Shannon tells us is child-friendly, and as we go inside I can hear the noise that three thousand kids make as they run riot.

Never mind about the adults having to shout to each other across the table, Ben's having a good time if nobody else is. There's an indoor play area that Anita takes him over to, and I've a feeling that when we get home she's going to want to take me up on my recent offer to start procreating. I don't mind doing the first bit, it's the following 20 years that's putting the wind up me.

Terry orders some beer while we wait for our food. Shannon tells me she's going to take Anita and Ben to the Westfield Centre tomorrow, because apparently my brother has a surprise for me. I look at Terry blankly, but he downs his pint in a couple of swallows and pretends he hasn't heard.

CHAPTER 35

TERRY STILL HASN'T said where we're going as we head into Sydney on the M5. The Clocktower car park in Harrington Street is giving nothing away as we park the car and start walking. After about 200 metres we reach a small office, and Terry gives me a wink and motions for me to follow him inside. He disappears over to Reception to check us in or do something or other, and I look at touristy pictures on the walls of people climbing up the Sydney Harbour Bridge.

It's only when the health and safety lecture begins that I realise we're actually going to climb up the bridge ourselves. Terry's silently pissing himself with laughter during the safety briefing as he looks sideways at me. However, I'm up for the challenge and give him a thumbs up, especially when I find out we'll be harnessed at all times. The boiler suits that we'll be wearing instead of our clothes look a bit dodgy, but hey, I ain't no fashionista.

I give silent thanks for the clear day and cool temperature as we follow the guide through a purpose-built tunnel underneath the bridge and start the 400 foot climb up the ladders and walkways to the top of the arch. I let Terry go first and kick his arse as he begins the ascent.

"Something tells me you've done this before."

"Yeah; a couple of times. There's a great view from the top."

I'm glad to see there's water stations and cooling fans, because pretty soon I'm starting to sweat. The guide wants to take our photos at every stop. I grab my brother and we pose in our boiler suits like two mongs on a day out.

The climb is slow and graded, and so I'm not too knackered when we reach the top. I have to admit the view is breath-taking; the sails of the opera house and downtown Sydney are over to the east, and Terry points out the Blue Mountains to the west and the dolphins swimming underneath the bridge. The guide leaves us be to savour the view, and I'm on a high up high with my brother. I sigh as I take it all in and feel the cold air on my face.

"I don't want to go home."

Terry shoots me a grin.

"Emigrate; come out here. It's a good life. You're young enough, you've got a skill, and now you've got family out here. You'll have no trouble getting in."

"Poor old Mum will be totally on her own. I admit I only see her at Easter and Christmas, but I'm there for emergencies. Also I don't know how Anita will feel about leaving her family behind."

"It's something you'll have to discuss with her." Terry nods sagely. "Of course I *had* to come out here. It's only a matter of time before somebody decides to dig up the patio in Miller Gardens to lay a lawn." He shrugs. "The old man had it coming; it was him or you, and I had to make sure it was *him*."

I don't know whether it's the high location, the

camaraderie, or the fact that I know my only brother will never let me down. I suddenly feel the need to get something off my chest to the one person who will always keep my secret.

"I've done the same thing."

There's no going back now. I see Terry turn towards me with a questioning look on his face.

"What?"

"I said I've done what you've done; I've killed somebody."

Terry laughs, but it sounds rather hollow.

"You're kidding, yeah?"

I watch a dolphin swimming around a boat passing under the bridge, and shake my head.

"No. I only wish I was, but I'm not."

My brother looks as stunned as I'm feeling. The disclosure suddenly makes it all seem more real.

"Who was he?"

"Not a he; *she* was a hooker that latched on to me. She ended up living with me. I couldn't get rid of her. She was even using my flat as a knocking shop while I was out at work, and I didn't know. The sex was great at first, but then I met Anita and this hooker…..she wouldn't go….."

"Fucking hell!" Terry exhales noisily.

I can't stop myself now; it's all got to come out.

"I asked a mate to clock me in at work so it looked like I'd taken a half hour lunch break. I took two hours instead and went home, intending to chuck out all her things on the pavement and change the locks. As far as I knew she usually went out somewhere during the day." I pause for breath and close my eyes against the strong breeze on my face. "As I was parking the car opposite my flat, there was a bloke coming out of it with a grin on his face. I unlocked the door and could hear her yelling from the bedroom. He'd left her handcuffed to the bed and she was furious, but not as angry as I was that she'd been using my bed to service her clients. I saw red; I knew she'd never go, and I wanted her out. I picked up a pillow and held it over her face. After that I left her there and went back to work. I don't know how I concentrated on anything else that afternoon."

Terry had been silent all the while, listening intently. He whistled softly as my diatribe came to an end, and acknowledged the guide signalling to us that we had 15 minutes left.

"Do the police suspect anything?"

"She had the client's DNA on her, and of course my fingerprints were all over the flat anyway. My *mate* couldn't resist the reward money being put up by the hooker's parents though, and told the police he'd clocked me in at work when I wasn't there. They looked over the timesheet records, but it's my word against his. According to the clock I only took half an hour for lunch. I've always had a temper, but Anita's calmed me down. I've even been to some of those anger management classes. The poor fuckers there are worse than I am."

Terry chuckled.

"Funny you should say that. I went to something similar to try and forget the old man and sort myself out when I first came over here. Can't say I feel any different though." He looked at me. "Does Anita know?"

"No." I shake my head. "It'd finish us if she knew."

"Your secret's safe with me." Terry looks at his watch. "Come on, let's go down. I know a great place in Darling Harbour where we can have some lunch."

PART 4 – ANITA
CHAPTER 36
AUGUST 2001

I'VE ONLY KNOWN Shannon for just over a week, but she's like the sister I never had. We seem to be on the same wavelength. We're both girly girls; we like shopping, make-up and clothes. Ben's adorable, and I've even changed my mind about waiting to have children. Shannon says it's best to have them while you're young, as you have more energy and are better equipped to deal with sleepless nights and the change in your routine.

Today the boys have gone out on the Manly scenic walkway. It's not easy with a toddler in tow and as much as possible I like to leave Paul to get to know his brother again, so instead Shannon is going to take me around The Rocks. Apparently it's a great place for shopping, and I need to find some presents and souvenirs to take back. We're meeting up with the boys later on for dinner, and it suits me just fine as I'm a little bit wary of Terry because of what I know he's done in the past. Of course he's the perfect gentleman all the time he's around me, but I wouldn't like to be on the other end of his temper. I can't ever imagine being angry enough to stick a carving knife in your own father. Paul's calmed down a lot lately and I'm glad, but then again Terry's actually killed somebody. I'd rather be out with Shannon and leave the boys to themselves.

We're going on the train into Sydney today, something that'll be a treat for Ben as well as for me. Shannon's let me dress Ben ready for the journey, and I'm beginning to realise how difficult it is to put clothes on somebody who won't keep still.

"You'll learn soon enough." Shannon laughs. "Give him a car to hold while you're doing up buttons; he loves cars."

"I'm just not used to three year olds." I stand up and laugh. "It's a whole new ball game."

Ben picks up on the conversation.

"Ball! I want a ball!"

"Auntie Anita will buy you one." I smile at him. "When we get to the shops."

We stop for coffee and a chat mid-morning while Ben has a nap. I push the buggy over towards an empty table in a far corner while Shannon joins the queue to order and pay. While I wait I get to thinking how nice it would be to live here and be able to meet up regularly for girly time with my new sister-in-law.

Shannon grins as she puts a fully laden tray down on the table and opens a bag, producing two blueberry muffins.

"One skinny latte for you, and one hot chocolate for me. And eat these before Ben wakes up."

"Lovely." I smile at her. "I'll get the next round."

We eat in companionable silence. However, I'm at a bit

of a loss as to how to reply when Shannon eventually speaks again.

"It seems strange that Terry left all his family behind to come over here. Until Paul sent him a message on Facebook he hadn't bothered getting in touch with any of you at all. Don't you think that's strange?"

I hedge around the question, aware that Shannon is watching my face intently.

"I don't really know Terry that well." I shrug. "Perhaps the boys had an argument before he left?"

"I think you know more than you're letting on. You might not know Terry, but you *do* know why he left though, don't you?"

Shannon's hazel eyes are mesmerising. I find myself blushing furiously, which does not go unnoticed by my sister-in-law.

"Come on; out with it. You *do* know why; I can see it in your face!"

She's smiling at me, but it's a false smile. I'm trapped in a corner and can't see a way out.

"Paul told me once, but he wouldn't want me to repeat anything."

Shannon slapped the table with the palm of her hand.

"I *knew* it! Come on; you've got to tell me. I'm his wife; it'll go no further I can assure you."

I look around in desperation as if one of the other customers in the café could help me in my moment of need. I look at Ben, still sleeping, in his pushchair in case by some stroke of luck he has woken up. I cannot seem to change the subject, and I've no idea what to do.

"I d-don't think it's a good idea." I shake my head.

"Anita....tell me! He's my husband, and I have a right to know!"

She's not too wrong there. If he ever flips again she or Ben might be in mortal danger. I suddenly reason that she has a right to know what her husband is really capable of.

"He killed his father." I whisper, looking around to make sure nobody is listening.

"What?" Shannon looks at me open-mouthed in disbelief.

"The guy had a baseball bat and was going to injure Paul, maybe kill him. Terry stabbed him with a carving knife to protect Paul."

Shannon's looking right through me as if I'm not there. I don't know whether I've done the right thing in telling her or not; she's got tears streaming down her face, and when I see them I wish I'd kept quiet.

"You're joking, right?" She sobs.

"I only wish I was."

I can't eat any more of my muffin; I'm suddenly not hungry anymore. Shannon asks one more question while wiping her eyes.

"What did they do with the body?"

I sigh and spill the beans. It's not worth holding anything else back.

"He's buried under the patio of their old house. He's never been found. His brother reported him missing after about a year, but Molly, his wife, was glad to see the back of him and told the police he'd gone off with another woman."

"Oh, my God" Shannon cries. "I just can't believe it!"

"It's true enough." I sigh. "Apparently he was violent and an alcoholic. I'm sure Paul's been scarred for life due to all the beatings he suffered as a kid; up until a few months' ago he had the same vicious temper."

Shannon blows her nose and tries to look as normal as you can look after hearing that your husband is a killer.

"Terry's always been so gentle with me and Ben. I'm having trouble getting my head around it all."

"Paul was in danger and Terry went to his rescue. That tells me a lot about Terry." I try to smooth things over. "He was doing the best for his brother."

The rest of the shopping trip falls flat, and I can't wait to meet up with the boys. Shannon takes Terry and Ben into their bedroom and closes the door after we all return home to get changed before going out for dinner. By the time Paul comes out of the shower there are raised voices filtering out into the hallway, Ben's wailing, and I'm pacing up and down wringing my hands. Paul puts on a clean shirt and Chinos, and indicates towards the door with his thumb.

"What's wrong? What's going on with them?"

I run to him, wanting him to make it all right again.

"I've done a terrible thing! I'm so sorry!" He holds me at arm's length.

"Just what are you going on about?"

At that moment our bedroom door bursts open and Terry, wild and agitated, appears and points a finger at me.

"You! You fucking little bitch! You just had to go and spoil it all, didn't you?"

I raise a hand to my mouth, frightened beyond belief. In my mind the moment will be forever frozen in aspic. Paul pushes me behind him and stands face-to-face in front his brother.

"Hey! Will someone tell me what the fuck is going on?"

From their bedroom I can hear Shannon sobbing. Ben begins pedalling one of his ride-on cars up and down the hallway, while Terry and Paul, recent comradeship forgotten, square up to each other like a pair of prize fighters.

"Your lovely wife told Shannon all about *Dad.*" Terry spits out the last word. "I moved ten thousand miles to get away and make a new life! Now thanks to Anita my wife thinks I'm some kind of serial killer!"

I see Shannon, still sobbing, run in and put her arms around Terry.

"It was my fault! I-I made her tell me! I always wondered why you came here and why you left all your family! You would never talk about it! Don't blame her; I made her do it!"

Terry breathes heavily and pushes Shannon away, all the while staring at me with eyes that would strike me dead in an instant if looks could kill. When he eventually does speak to me again, my blood runs cold.

"Here's one for you. Ask little brother here who killed the hooker in his bed. If he doesn't tell you, then I will! After all, *you've* caused my marriage to go tits up, so I don't see why yours shouldn't go the same way!"

Paul lashes out at Terry with a punch, who then retaliates before grabbing Shannon and slamming the bedroom door behind them so forcefully that the whole house seems to shake. I run and throw the bolt home, although I'm certain Terry could kick down the door with no trouble if he chose to do so. I turn around and face Paul.

"Is it true? Did you kill Catherine Taylor?"

Paul, fists bunched and red-faced with fury, towers over me.

"How could you do something like that to them? Are you stupid, or what?"

The holiday which had been going so well, has now spiralled down into a seething mass of hatred. I thought Shannon might have been proud of Terry protecting Paul the way he did. Paul slaps my face so hard that my bladder gives way spontaneously, and a stream of hot pee soaks into the carpet. I sob and crumple to the floor, curling up into a ball to protect myself. I can hear Paul breathing heavily above me, and I blurt out the only thing I can think of.

"I'm so sorry!"

He doesn't reply straight away, and I wait for a possible kick in the ribs until I hear the bedsprings shift as he flops down. I stay where I am.

"It's a bit late for that, isn't it?"

His voice has lost its fury. I look up and he has his head in his hands, sitting on the edge of the bed. I stumble into the en-suite and lock the door, needing to get away from him and take my wet things off. I stand under the shower and let the cool water take away the stinging on my face. When I come out into the bedroom wrapped in a towel he's still in the same position, looking down on the floor. I put on some clean clothes, grab my bag, phone and purse, throw back the bolt, and run towards the front door, wanting to be anywhere other than where I am at that particular moment.

It is early evening and people are coming home from work. I wrap my jacket around me and walk the route into Liverpool that we've previously taken in the car. I've no idea what I'll do when I get there, but the relief at being away from the house is overwhelming. I have to face the fact that my husband killed Catherine Taylor and has a temper he cannot control, and could possibly kill again if he becomes angry enough. I realise that my dad's instincts about Paul had been right all along. I know my marriage is over now, and that I'll have to go straight to DC Elliott as soon as I return home. I feel an absolute fool for accepting Paul's lies as the truth all this time. I also realise as I walk along that he never replied to my question about whether he actually did kill her, but I already know the answer to that in my heart of hearts.

After about half an hour I come to Memorial Avenue, and sink down onto a bench to let the world go by. I close my eyes and relish the cool breeze on my face. I am 10,000 miles from home, in a strange town, staying with a husband and brother-in-law who are killers and who now both hate me. My passport and airline ticket are in my bag, but my flight home is not for another 5 days.

The night is fast approaching. My phone begins to ring, but I have burned my boats and have no intention of ever returning to the house. I stand up and pace along Memorial Avenue, realising with dismay that the amount of money I have in my purse will not last very long if I have to rent a hotel room. As I blindly walk on I come to the conclusion there is only one thing left that I *can* do.

I ask a passing pedestrian where I can find the police station, and she points me in the direction of Flowerdale Road, telling me to turn second right into Moore Street. Flowerdale Road seems to stretch on for ages and I step up my pace, looking at nobody and eager to reach a place of safety. However, as I pass Anderson Avenue I am conscious that a car has stopped on the road in front of me. Dismayed, I see Paul getting out of the passenger seat. Terry is behind the wheel, but he too climbs out of the car and both of them stand in front of me on the pavement.

"Go away!" I try to sidestep them.

Paul comes forward and holds out his arms.

"We've been driving around for ages looking for you. Come back; I'm sorry I hit you. We can work this out. Where are you going?"

"Nowhere." I lie. "I'm just walking."

Terry shakes his head and comes to stand beside Paul.

"The police station is just around the corner. She knows where she's going alright."

I'm cornered; stuck with two men who have been brutalised for long enough during their childhood to think that murder might be a viable option at any time in order to achieve their aims.

There's no way I can outrun the pair of them. I sigh and let them lead me back to the car, safe in the knowledge that I can contact the police on my return to the UK, unless Paul decides to hold me prisoner for the rest of my life.

CHAPTER 37

BY THE TIME we get back to the house Ben is bathed and in bed, and Shannon, bless her, has rustled up some salmon steaks and vegetables. There's a terrible atmosphere as the four of us sit around the table, and I for one intend to eat the meal in total silence so as not to be the cause of any more arguments.

I keep my eyes firmly fixed on my plate as I eat. I'm halfway through my dinner when Terry breaks the silence.

"Look; Anita, I'm sorry for shouting at you. Shannon says she forced you to tell her. I suppose I've always been stupid enough to think that she would never find out. You've done me a favour really but I was too blind to see it earlier on. There are no secrets between us now, and Shannon accepts that I was trying to protect Paul at the time."

"Sorry I put pressure on you to tell me, Anita." Shannon briefly rested her hand on top of mine. "Terry is the man for me, and he's a great father to Ben. I'm going to assume that you won't be taking this any further."

Paul, who so far hasn't spoken, glances sideways at me, waiting for my answer. I shrug, carry on looking down, and resist catching anybody's eye.

"No, Shannon. I'm not going to break up your family." I mumble, with a mouth full of salmon. "I promise I won't do anything that does that."

All three of them beam at me. Terry, upbeat and looking a great deal happier, puts down his knife and fork and takes a sip of wine.

"Let's all make a pact here and now that what we know stays between us four and us four only, and that we never speak of it again. What says all of you?"

"Done." Paul is first to answer.

"Of course." Shannon agrees.

"Yes." I nod.

An almost palpable *frisson* of relief shoots around the table as we all join hands, and I lie through my teeth to save my own skin. I find I now cannot stand the sight of Paul, who grins and begins to shovel food into his mouth like it's going out of fashion. I baulk at the upcoming drama I know will be taking place in our room later on, and increase my resolve not to fall for his charms this time.

After dinner I watch TV with the others and make desultory small talk. I think all four of us are relieved when I eventually plead exhaustion and make a move towards the bedroom. I feign sleep when Paul comes in some time later, undresses, and climbs into bed beside me.

"Anita, I *know* you're awake."

I am so uptight that I've forgotten to breathe heavily. I am lying next to a murderer, and at the touch of his hand on my skin I find I want to recoil, jump out of the window, and keep on running. However, I turn over so that my back is towards him, and I let it be known the only way I know how that I am deeply and utterly revolted by his very being.

"Fuck off. If you hit me again *I'll* be the one sticking *you* with the carving knife."

The bed rocks as Paul reaches out and turns on the bedside lamp.

"You don't mean that. Look; I'm sorry I hit you. I was angry with you for spilling the beans to Shannon, and then Terry came in and shot his mouth off. I was all over the place; I'm sorry. It'll never happen again."

I sigh, sit up, and look at him.

"Yes it will, Paul, because you can't control your anger. You think it's normal to go around murdering people because they're not doing what you want? Poor Catherine Taylor! You're a monster! I married a monster for God's sake!"

I begin to weep as I lay back down on the pillow. All I ever wanted was a decent husband to love me and a normal family of my own. Instead I seem to have acquired Edinburgh's answer to Jack the Ripper.

Paul cuddles up behind me and puts one arm around my waist. I flinch at his touch, and try to project my mind away from my current predicament. I can feel his breath on the back of my neck as he speaks.

"Let me know how I can make it up to you. You'll never see me raise a hand to you ever again. I love you; I only want us to be happy."

I realise I'm going to have to cast my mind back to my college days and bring all my acting skills to the fore so as not to alarm him. I sigh and pat his hand as it encircles my middle; the hand that has suffocated Catherine Taylor.

"I do love you Paul, but your anger frightens me."

I can hear the relief in his voice as he answers.

"I adore you. I'll never hurt you again. Like Terry and

Shannon, there will never be any more secrets between us. We'll have lots of children, and I'll never even shout at them, let alone do anything else."

I ignore the fact that he's talking out of his arse. At his words I silently cry myself to sleep with the realisation of what I'm going to have to do.

Fingers of sunlight are dappling the room when I'm awakened at 07:45 by Paul bringing me in some tea and toast. He has a fixed grin on his face and I quickly remember to go along with the pretence of being a happy wife until I can grab the chance to visit DC Elliott. We still have four more days of holiday left, and I tell myself to go with the flow and enjoy whatever Terry and Shannon have in store for us.

"Thanks." I give him what passes for a smile and take the tray. "You didn't need to do that."

Paul jumps into bed again and plants a kiss on my cheek.

"Nothing but the best is good enough for my girl."

I chew on the toast and drink the tea whilst thinking about the cuddle I have to get through which I know Paul will expect to lead the way to sex. I grit my teeth as I finish my breakfast and place the tray on the bedside table, letting him pull my head towards his shoulder.

"I love you, baby. I'm sorry about yesterday."

"So am I." I state truthfully, knowing my short marriage is over. "Let's begin again."

He moves on top of me; his erection already evident. As I wrap my legs around him I think about Catherine Taylor, snuffed out in the prime of her life by my pig of a husband. I will have to ensure that I'm not the next one on his list.

CHAPTER 38

IT'S 9TH AUGUST already, my 19th birthday, and Paul's bought me a lovely necklace with matching earrings. As a treat I get to pick where we go today. I suggest that a trip to Sydney wouldn't be complete without a visit to Bondi Beach, although Terry does tell me that August is not the best time of the year to see it in all its glory. However, everybody's up for it, and after breakfast I help Shannon to find Ben's bucket and spade, and we tog him up for the cold weather. Paul is Mr Affable himself, as he jokes with Terry, talks to Ben, and cuddles me in the back of the car.

On arrival I can see the surfers having a great time of it in the chilly waters, dressed appropriately in their rubber suits. We set up camp on the sand, all dressed for winter. Terry and Paul keep warm by kicking a ball to each other, and Shannon and I help Ben to make sandcastles. We're all careful not to upset the proverbial apple cart, and Terry especially goes out of his way to be extra nice, bringing back five portions of fish and chips for lunch from a takeaway café near the beach.

We sit in our deckchairs and eat in a kind of companionable silence. Paul checks that I'm not too cold, and offers me his jacket. I shake my head and carry on watching the surfers, wanting desperately to be home with Mum to bask in her garden in the heat of an August afternoon without a care in the world.

Shannon screws up her greasy takeaway paper and gives Ben a drink.

"Is this all the British eat? Fish and chips?"

"No." Paul replies. "Sometimes we just eat chips without the fish."

"Paul, d'you recall waiting at the end of Miller Gardens on a Friday night for Len the Fish as a kid?" Terry laughs. "Remember his greaseball van? God knows what he fried those chips in."

I hear Paul laugh.

"Yeah, it's a wonder we've survived this long without a heart attack."

"Was Miller Gardens in Edinburgh?" I ask. "Was it your childhood home? There's so much more about Paul that I've got to learn."

"That's right." Terry chomps on a large chip. "Number forty eight was right at the other end of the road. By the time we'd got home to Mum with the grub, we'd always eaten all the chips and she'd give us a right bollo…..."

"Terry!" Shannon admonishes and looks at Ben. "He repeats everything he hears!"

"Sorry; yeah, Mum would shout at us and make us pay for another portion of chips just for her out of our pocket money."

I laugh as heartily as I can.

Never have I been so glad to be able to go home.   Paul doesn't murmur as he takes a load of my stuff into his case so that I can close the lid.

"Have you had a good time?"

He looks at me hopefully in a sort of childlike fashion. I decide to make his day.

"Yes I have. I've been thinking…..shall I come off the pill soon so that we can try for a baby?"

He rushes over to me and holds me tight. I can feel his heart hammering away. However, all I can think of is Catherine's dead heart lying still in her coffin, and I know I'm doing the right thing.

"Sweetheart, you don't know how I've been longing for you to say that!"

He kisses me and I wonder how soon I can use morning sickness as an excuse not to go to work for the day.

I hate airport goodbyes. I've come to like Shannon, and as I roll out the platitudes about meeting up for a second time next year, I'm sad at the certainty that our paths will never again cross in the future. I hug Ben's little body close, imagining a new-born baby of my own, but then shudder at the thought of bringing a child of Paul's into the world. After a few weeks of suffering the effects of sleepless nights, I know Paul would be on such a short fuse that I could never leave a screaming baby alone with him for even one moment.

Terry hugs me briefly and then turns his attention to Paul, whispering something in his ear that Shannon and I are not privy to. I watch the brothers hugging, and I'm surprised to see that Paul has tears in his eyes. As we queue up for a security check at the entrance to the departure lounge I take one last look backwards and notice Terry watching me grimly, his eyes glittering.

"Are you okay?" I turn to Paul.

"Yeah." He wipes away some tears quickly. "Why wouldn't I be?"

He's quiet as we take a last look around the Duty Free shops. I get some perfume for Mum and some after-shave for Dad before we wander off and find something to eat. Paul picks at his food which is worrying in itself, as he usually eats like a hog at a trough. I bite into a burger and risk the question I've been longing to ask.

"What did Terry say to you back there when he whispered in your ear?"

Paul lays down his knife and fork and smiles at me in an odd way.

"He told me to keep an eye on you."

"Keep an eye on me?" I ignore the heartsink moment. "Why?"

"He doesn't trust you, but I told him you wouldn't be so stupid as to go to the police." He stares at me. "You wouldn't; would you?"

The threat is there, veiled in a genial manner, but still there all the same. I suffer a stab of terror amongst the busy to-ing and fro-ing of passengers behind us in an airport that never sleeps.

"Don't be silly! Paul, we made a pact never to talk about the subject again. As far as I know we're going home to try for a baby, aren't we?"

He relaxes a little and looks more like his normal self.

"Of course we are. I told Terry he was talking bullshit anyway."

When we stand up to make our way to the gate for boarding, my legs seem to have turned to jelly.

CHAPTER 39

ONE MONDAY MORNING at the end of October I figure I can start to put my plan into action. When I can feel that Paul is awake beside me I stumble out of bed, run to the bathroom, pour some salt into a cup of warm water, say a quick prayer, and drink the lot.

The vomiting is prolonged and noisy. Paul runs in to stroke my back and keep my hair away from my face. Weak and wretched, I flush the toilet and sink to the floor.

"I think I'm pregnant; my period's late."

He hugs me and has trouble keeping the excitement out of his voice.

"Stay at home today. I'll tell Doddy you're not well."

"Don't bother phoning to check on me; I'm fine, really. I just want to go back to sleep."

I slink into bed and rest until he leaves the flat to go to work. As soon as he's gone I get up, have a shower, and chew on some toast to line my stomach. At 09:30 I'm walking into town on a pleasant autumn day, as nervous as hell, but certain that I'm doing the right thing.

The policewoman on duty at the desk looks up from the computer and smiles at me.

"Hello. Can I help?"

"I need to speak to DC Elliott please."

"Who shall I say is asking?" She looks at me with interest.

"Tell him it's Paul McAdam's wife Anita."

Within a few moments a burly middle aged man comes out and introduces himself as DC Elliott. I'm shown into a side room and given a cup of tea. Pleasantries over, he takes out a notebook and looks at me.

"Now then, Mrs McAdam. What can I do for you?" I'm so terrified that my voice is shaking as I speak. "You've been after the person who killed Catherine Taylor last year."

"Yes." He nods and sits up straighter.

"Well, I can tell you that my husband murdered her. You won't be able to prove it, but hopefully there'll be some evidence to arrest him for his father's murder instead. I think there might be some DNA on the knife he used."

The policeman is silent for a moment before standing up and grabbing a recording machine out of a cupboard.

"You don't mind if I record this interview, do you?"

I shake my head.

"No; I don't mind at all."

I have managed to get his attention straight away. I want to get it all over with and return to the flat in case Paul slips home for lunch. DC Elliott turns on the recorder, states the time, date, and our names, and then sits back in his chair.

"Carry on Mrs McAdam."

"From information I've learned over the past couple of months, I can tell you that Paul's father, Ian McAdam, was stabbed to death and is lying ten feet under a patio at forty eight Miller Gardens here in Edinburgh."

DC Elliott looks directly at me.

"Who gave you this information?"

I keep the eye contact.

"Paul himself, but I had to pick the right time to disclose it. Apparently the murder took place nearly five years ago. The house is Paul's childhood home; his mother now lives elsewhere, but I think she always assumed her husband had gone off with another woman. Paul has also confessed to suffocating Catherine Taylor, but I don't think there's any proof of that."

"I see."

"Mr Elliott, over the past year or so I've discovered that my husband isn't the person I thought I'd married. He has a terrible temper, and I'm in fear of my life. If he's arrested and let go again I dread to think what he'll do to me. I know I'm telling you your job here, but you must gather the evidence first before you arrest him. If the Press get wind of it, perhaps tell them something about the new owners finding the body when they dug up the patio to lay a new lawn. Nobody must know that I've given you this information." I remember Terry's words to Paul at the airport, and I shudder. "My life might be in danger otherwise."

I notice a small flash of annoyance pass over the policeman's face, which is soon masked by his professional manner.

"In danger from whom, might I ask?"

I recall the mental image of Terry's eyes boring into mine at the departure lounge.

"From my husband if he ever gets out of prison, and from anybody else he knows who might have no qualms about carrying out his wishes if he's in prison and wants to bump me off out of revenge."

"Don't worry, Mrs McAdam. You have been very brave in coming here to see me. We have your husband's DNA samples taken on the day Catherine Taylor was murdered. Leave it to us; we'll be investigating forty eight Miller Gardens quite soon."

It's quarter past eleven when I leave the police station. When I get home I remember to take another contraceptive pill to keep my period at bay. I make myself a sandwich around twelve o'clock, and then sink down onto the sofa with a cup of tea just as my phone rings.

"Hi Paul!" I try to sound cheerful.

"Hey, beautiful. How are you feeling?"

"Okay now. I've just had a sandwich. Tell Doddy I'll be in this afternoon."

"Great. Will do."

I'm on a high as I drive into the office. I've carried out my promise not to incriminate Terry, who after all was only trying to protect his brother. Hopefully Molly will not need to be involved too much, and she'll read the concocted story in the newspapers. The plan is all going rather well, just as I'd hoped it would.

I'm on tenterhooks all the time, waiting for the police to turn up. Paul thinks I'm excited about the pregnancy, and starts talking about buying a pram, cot, and high chair. I tell him to wait until I'm a little further along just to make sure. My so-called visits to the doctor's surgery for 'ante-natal' check-ups give me time to pop into the police station, where DC Elliot tells me that they have found the body, and are working on recovering enough DNA evidence from the scene. The Press are under strict instructions not to let the story out.

One thing I have no control over is the phone call Paul makes to his brother to tell him that he's going to become a father. I have a sinking feeling in my stomach as Paul relates the news. He then phones Molly, who is understandably over the moon that she will soon be a grandmother. She has no idea of Ben's existence, and I am under strict instructions from Paul not to tell her.

It's early morning on the 14th November 2001 when we're woken by a loud knocking on the front door. Paul throws on some jeans and a t-shirt and is arrested and charged with his father's murder as he stands there bewildered and blinking in the hallway, getting read his rights but calling out my name like a lost child crying for its mother. I shed real tears of anguish for the end of my marriage and an uncertain future for myself as I hug him before he is led away.

I take matters into my own hands, phone Molly, and let her know that the current owners of her old house found the body of her husband in the garden when they dug up the patio. Her voice sounds surprised, even more so when I tell her that Paul has been charged with the murder.

I move out of Paul's flat and stay temporarily with Dad and Tricia. I feel somehow safer there. I inform my father that he was right about Paul all along, but bless him, he doesn't utter those four words *I told you so* that I'm waiting for. I tell Mum that I'll be giving up my job and moving back with her when the trial is over and the police are done with me. She cries on the phone, and so do I.

I carry on working at Dodd's, but put Christmas aside as the date for Paul's trial in mid-December draws nearer. I've been allowed a couple of visits, and I go along for old time's sake. I'm surprised when he tells me he's been working with a wonderful prison counsellor, the kind of which he realises he should have had access to as a teenager. He seems a broken man when I tell him the shock of his arrest has caused me to miscarry. He cries and reaches out to me through the security glass. I can see he's lost weight, and he begs me to get in touch with Terry and let him know what is going on. He tells me he's written a letter to his brother and left a message on his answerphone, but so far has received no reply. I am of the opinion that Terry and Shannon have probably disappeared to evade a possible future visit from the Australian police, but I do not want to make him any more depressed than he already is. I also fail to tell him that I will be filing for a divorce in the very near future.

CHAPTER 40

THE IMPOSING SURROUNDINGS of the Crown Court and the sight of the judge, jury and barristers bring it home to me just what I've done to my husband as I take a seat with Dad in the public gallery. Paul is brought in wearing a prison uniform and looks thin and pale as he takes a seat in-between two security guards in the dock. His eyes seek mine and he looks at me pleadingly, like a lost soul. A long line of Press are busy writing; polishing up the articles which will no doubt appear in tomorrow's tabloids.

The first day of the trial is taken up with the swearing in of the jury, and the defence and prosecution's opening speeches. Being Paul's wife I've not been called on to give any evidence, and to be honest I'm grateful for not being required to stand up and speak in front of such an august gathering.

DC Elliott is sworn in on the second day to give evidence for the prosecution. Straight away he announces he received information from a reliable source that Ian McAdam's body was buried under a patio at 48 Miller Gardens. Without looking over at Paul I can sense his eyes are boring into mine from the dock, and that he knows without a doubt just who the 'reliable source' is. I keep my eyes fixed on the floor as the defence barrister asks DC Elliott to reveal the source of the information, but I'm somewhat relieved when the policeman declines and states instead that to disclose the person's identity could possibly put them in fear of their life.

Mitchell Land, a forensics expert, is the prosecution's next witness. He confirms that DNA from Paul and also a similar type of DNA that he presumes is from a sibling was found on the carving knife which had been buried with Ian McAdam's body. He tells the court quite confidently he has no doubt that Paul, and probably one other person related to him, carried out the murder.

The prosecution seem to have done their homework well when I hear Darren Maynard's name called out. I hadn't seen Darren in quite a while since he left Dodd's, but now he seems eager to talk, telling the jury how Paul had assaulted him and how his former friend was fiery, short-tempered, and quick with his fists. I risk a quick glance at Paul when Darren steps down, and he looks as though all the stuffing has been knocked out of him.

I'm more interested in the defence case, which takes place on the third day. I'm surprised beyond belief when the first person called in to give evidence is none other than my mother-in-law. Molly, ignoring possible prosecution herself, never takes her eyes from her son as she tells the jury how Paul was frequently the victim of his father's violent temper. She describes in vivid detail the beatings and lashings with a belt which left weals on her son's back for days and which she was too weak to prevent. I listen spellbound as dry-eyed and with a clear voice, she states the fact that Ian McAdam always suspected that Paul was not his son, and after he'd been drinking often took his frustrations out on the boy. However, she adds firmly that Paul is his son, as she only ever had physical relations with one man, and that man was Ian McAdam.

Paul looks at his mother intently throughout her statement. I realise I'd never known the extent of the punishment which Paul had endured as a child and young teenager, and at that moment my heart goes out to him. I want him to look over at me so that I can convey some sort of sympathy, but his eyes are fixed on his mother.

Molly goes on to state that she watched her eldest son Terry stabbing his father as Ian McAdam was about to strike Paul on the head with a baseball bat, and that Terry stabbed his father to protect his brother. She tells the jury how she knew where the body had been buried, but had taken so many beatings herself from her husband that she was happy not to report him missing. As an afterthought she adds that Paul and Terry buried the body and the knife together; digging a hole in the garden undercover of night, and eventually laying a patio on top. Molly tells how Terry disappeared to Australia after the stabbing, and how she hasn't seen or heard from him since and has no idea of his whereabouts.

The jury seem just as stunned as I am. Even Dad doesn't say a word. I look at Paul smiling at Molly, and see the bond between a mother and son which can never be broken. It looks to me as if the trial might go somewhere to rekindle their relationship in the future. I'm pleased for him that at least there will always be somebody on his side, but feel guilty when I know that it's not going to be me anymore.

I'm surprised when the defence swear in Christine Lessing, the prison counsellor who has been working with Paul. Christine is a forty-something no-nonsense lady, who reminds me of a lecturer I had at college. She takes the stand and states how she has been working with Paul on anger management issues on a daily basis during his prison confinement. I'm fascinated when she addresses the jury to say that the beatings, lashings, and lack of care from his father which he suffered as a child when he was powerless and helpless have caused the feelings of anger he currently experiences as an adult, as he is now able to strongly assert himself. However, she goes on to say that Paul is now aware of what is causing his anger, has been a model pupil, and has been dedicating himself to learning coping strategies.

I must admit, even looking briefly at Paul sitting in the dock I can tell that he seems a different person. No longer is there any cocky swagger to his demeanour; he seems altogether more serene and composed. He sends me a thin smile, and I find myself responding with a smile of my own.

Last up for the defence is Bernard Dobbs, who swears an oath on the bible and states that Paul is skilled at his job of a technical support officer, is a good worker, and always volunteers for any overtime. He adds while looking up at Paul that he has never needed to discipline him for bad timekeeping, bad behaviour, or discourtesy to other staff. I'm flabbergasted when Mr Dobbs states in a loud voice that he would be happy to have Paul back working at Dobbs &Co any time.

When Paul takes the stand he looks at me and apologises

profusely for all the times his anger got the better of him. The tone of his voice is even and non-confrontational as he answers all the questions the prosecution and defence put to him. He admits to helping his brother to bury Ian McAdam's body, and says that with hindsight he realises his father had the same anger management issues, which were compounded by an extreme addiction to alcohol. When he steps down I feel like applauding his performance.

PART 5 – PAUL
CHAPTER 41
DECEMBER 2001

NEVER IN MY wildest dreams did I expect to get let off with 300 hours of community service. I'm abso-fucking-lutely made up. I step down from the dock and my hands are shaking as I reach out and thank my barrister, Christine, dear old Doddy, and my mum, who I'm hoping against hope isn't going to be prosecuted herself for being an accessory to murder. I'm virtually a free man, but after checking in my pockets I realise I have no keys to my flat on me, and no money to get home. There's only one person who will have a spare set of keys and who can give me a lift; my wife.

Anita. The girl I'll love until they put the last nail in my coffin. I've been such a shit to her, and to women in general in the past. Christine has made me see what repressed anger from childhood can do to a person. When I think of how I suffocated Cat it's like I'm reliving the actions of another man, an angry one who had nothing much to live for. I could have confessed to Cat's murder whilst standing there in the dock, but hey, would you if you thought there was a chance that you might be able to atone for your sins by removing graffiti or sweeping the roads instead of rotting away in a cell for the rest of your life? I also don't blame Terry for disappearing. He's got Ben and Shannon to look after now, and they mean the world to him.

I can see her coming towards me. Her father is hanging back in the public gallery looking like he's lost a tenner and found five pence, but at least Anita is walking over to congratulate me. I want to hug her close, but stop myself.

"Good news, eh?"

"Absolutely." She smiles. "Are you okay for getting home?"

"Er…no." I shrug. "I've got no keys to get in, and no money."

"Dad'll give you a lift." She looks down. "I'm….living with Dad and Tricia at the moment."

"I don't blame you for that. Perhaps when I've done my community service you might think about moving back in and giving us another go?"

"I don't think so." She shakes her head. "I want to file for a divorce actually. I'm going to move back to London eventually and start college again next September."

My world falls apart at that moment, but the only person I've got to blame is myself. Welcome to my nightmare.

The flat is cold and empty without Anita. All the food in the fridge has gone bad, and there's something black growing on the inside of the fridge door. I sigh; it looks like I'll be walking down to the chippy tonight then for my tea.

The phone rings; it's Derek, my Community Payback Supervisor making his presence felt already. He wants to meet up tomorrow. I tell him I'll be at work during the day, but that I can see him in the evening. He says he has a long list of jobs to keep me occupied after work every day. Whoop-de-fucking-do-dah, or 'Squeeze me, Jimmy Johnson, squeeze me,' as my delightful father used to say when he could talk coherently. I ruminate on the last sentence; who the bloody hell was Jimmy Johnson anyway?

I don't want to live in a tomb. I turn up the central heating, clean the fridge out, and even hoover round to keep busy and stop myself thinking about Anita. I'm knocked out after a high-fat supper of battered plaice and chips, and don't even bother moving off the settee to get into bed. When I wake up at 05:30 I'm still fully clothed and laying in front of the TV, which is showing one of those awful shopping channels; a voice tells everyone what Christmas gifts they can buy for their nearest and dearest. That's okay then; not having anybody can save me some money there.

I want to pick up Doddy and squeeze him as I clock in, but manage to restrain myself. Everyone pretends I've been on a little holiday, and I let it be known straight off that I'm up for any overtime going unless I have a community service job to do in the evenings. I keep my nose to the grindstone all day, and barely speak to a soul. I see Anita in the canteen at lunchtime, but she's sitting with a new girl. When I take my tray over to an empty table, she walks by me on her way out and gives me what passes for a smile.

"Okay?"

"Sure." I shrug. "How's yourself?"

"Not too bad." She glances around to see who's looking at us. "I'm training Julie up to take over my job. I've given

Doddy a month's notice."

"Great." I take a bite of a sandwich. "Hope everything works out for you."

Her father has obviously poisoned the one remaining corner of her mind that might have retained some feelings for me. I notice she's not wearing her wedding or engagement rings anymore either. Looks like the horse's arse has finally been kicked out to pasture.

Derek's not a bad bloke actually. I give him a beer when he comes round later that evening, and he measures me up for one of those high-vis orange jackets with *Community Service* written on the back. My nightmare is now complete. I ask him whether mum is going to be prosecuted, but he says he's heard on the grapevine that she could possibly be let off with a fine as she failed to report a crime of passion murder that she was an accessory to, not a pre-meditated murder.

It seems the first job I've got is creosoting some graffiti-covered fencing surrounding the park where Anita and I once sat freezing our arses off watching some mates play a game of football. Seeing as it's nearly Christmas and it's dark at four o'clock in the afternoon, Derek says I can work all weekend at it instead. Super; it beats sitting across the road in the Rat and Pigeon, passing the time of day with Ray, and quietly soaking at the bar. Derek's even going to turn up at the park to bring me the creosote and ensure that I make a start on it. How's that for service?

The local wankers are out in force on that first Saturday, taking the piss out of my jacket and asking who I've murdered. In the old days I would have taken great pleasure in shutting them up with a kicking, but Christine's voice is in my head telling me to project my mind away to a pleasant activity. I apply the creosote with even strokes and imagine I'm caressing Anita's naked body with the paintbrush. It works; the jeers and jibes stop eventually, but I get a bugger of a hard-on.

I can't feel my fingers by the time it starts to get dark. I take off my fashionable jacket, pack up the empty tins of creosote, and leave them all in the car and head into the Rat and Pigeon. Ray gives me a thumbs up.

"How's the painting going?"

"I'll finish it over Christmas; I've got nothing else to do."

"Good on ya; you'll get through it. Have this one on me."

The beer's frothy and welcome, especially as it's free. It occurs to me that I could be festering in a prison cell instead, and so enjoy my surroundings, even if it *is* only the Rat and Pigeon.

Derek says I don't have to work on Christmas Day, and to be honest, I think it's time to go and see my old mum. I phone her on Christmas Eve; she sounds pleased and tells me to come round the next day for lunch. It's not my ideal way to spend Christmas Day, but I suppose it beats sitting in the flat on my own.

There's a pleasant surprise around 10 o'clock on the morning of the big day. The doorbell rings and when I answer it Anita's standing there with a present. I look at her as though she's grown three heads. Her voice, however, is music to my ears.

"Aren't you going to ask me in then?"

I remember that I'm trying to be one of those perfect gentlemen you see posing on the covers of knitting patterns.

"Sorry; of course. Come in."

Only a few months' ago she was living here, and now she has to ask permission to come in. She looks good enough to eat. I follow behind her as she makes herself comfortable on the settee.

"I didn't like to think of you sitting here alone today."

I'm no charity case, and I don't need pity. I shake my head.

"I'm not; I'm going to my mum's for lunch later on."

"Oh good." Anita smiles. "I bought you a little something."

I have a Christmas present. I turn it over in my hands and look at her.

"I haven't bought *you* anything I'm afraid. I've been busy creosoting down the park or working overtime, and anyway, I didn't expect to see you today."

"That's okay. I just wanted to give you a present to say no hard feelings."

I tear off the paper and it's a framed photo of Terry, Shannon and Ben that she must have taken on Bondi Beach with her phone. At that moment I realise I miss my brother so much that it actually hurts.

"Cheers." I swallow and blink back tears as I look down at it. "It's a lovely present."

All I have left of my brother is this photo that I'll treasure. I close my eyes and take a deep breath, but it's no good. I'm too choked up to say anything else.

"Sorry to make you upset." Anita shuffles over to me on the settee. "That wasn't my intention."

I swallow hard again, think of creosoting, and manage to keep a lid on my emotions. When I'm sure my voice will not come out sounding like an adolescent schoolboy's I risk a reply.

"You're a good girl, Anita; the best. I'll give you the divorce; don't worry. You deserve somebody better than me."

She squeezes my hands, stands up, and makes for the door.

"Dad's waiting outside in the car." She whispers. "Merry Christmas."

Even my mum looks pleased to see me today. It occurs to me that I haven't bought her a present, but then again I expect she hasn't bought me one either. I give her a quick hug at the door and then enter the flat.

"The turkey smells good."

"It's a chicken crown actually. Turkeys are too big; I'd end up still eating it at Easter."

I stand in the kitchen doorway, watch her bustling about, and realise that I don't really know her; my own mother. Why did she stay with my bastard of a father for so long?

"Thanks for speaking up for me in the court." I take a seat at the table. "I'm sure it was you who swayed the jury."

Mum takes the chicken out of the oven.

"What else can a mother do for her son? I've heard nothing from the court yet, but I don't care about any punishment for myself, just as long as you got off. How's the community service going?"

"I'm ace with the creosoting brush." I laugh. "Stand still for long enough and I'll creosote *you*."

Her face breaks into a grin. It's such a rare sight that I'm stupefied for a moment. She suddenly looks twenty years younger.

"How's Anita?"

"Okay I think." I shrug my shoulders. "She wants a divorce."

"That's a shame." Mum carves the chicken and serves up the vegetables. "I'd taken quite a shine to her."

"She deserves better; I've got too much of my father in me."

On hearing my words, Mum turns around and faces me.

"No you haven't; you're not his son! You can change your life around; don't hold on to old grievances. Move on and get your girl back."

She turns and carries on preparing the dinner, but I'm left stupefied.

"What? Dad *wasn't* my father?" I get up from the table, walk over to her, and look her in the eyes.

"No, he wasn't, but he provided for us and I had nowhere else to go. My pregnancy with you was the result of a wonderful affair that I'll remember until the end of my days."

You could strike me down with a feather. The old man had known it all along, but Mum had kept Terry and I in the dark. Everything was making sense; in fact, I would go as far as to say that I'd never felt as close to my mum as I did at that very moment. The empathy makes me venture into unknown territory.

"What was my dad's name?"

Mum gives a sigh and has a faraway look in her eyes.

"Richard Ellis. Paul was his middle name. He liked to be called Ricky. Keep it to yourself though; I don't want anybody to think badly of me."

I shake my head in wonder.

"Of course I won't say anything, but why the hell did you and dad marry in the first place?"

Mum gives a wry laugh as she prepares the gravy.

"He wasn't like it when we first got together, as he wasn't an alcoholic then. Little did I know that he was working on it. By the time Terry was born, our marriage was a farce."

I can't help it. I reach out and give her a hug.

"Wasn't there a refuge you could have gone to?"

"I tried that; he found me and I had the beating of my life."

I stick my neck out a bit more.

"Where did you meet my real dad? Don't you want to try and find him again?"

Mum shakes her head again.

"He was married with children. He was the manager of a residential home I worked in at weekends when Terry was small. I loved him, but I didn't want to break up his home and leave his children without a father."

"Where did the two of you work then?" I ask with interest.

"At The Beeches in Elderslie Street."

"You're going to see me a lot more often." I kiss the top of her head. "I'm sorry I've been such a shit son."

"No, Paul." Mum breaks away and pours gravy onto our plates. "It's the other way around. I couldn't protect you. It's me who's to blame here."

I carry the plates to the table and smile at her.

"I've been in touch with Terry on Facebook. I printed out a photo of him, his wife Shannon and their son Ben that he put on his Facebook page. I'll copy it for you and bring it round in the week."

Mum looks at me misty-eyed.

"Terry's been in touch?" She whispers.

I thought it best to omit my visit to Australia. I nod and spear a piece of chicken with my fork.

"You've got a little grandson, Ben. He's three. Of course I've no idea where Terry lives; we're just in contact on Facebook."

Mum looks fit to burst with happiness.

"I have a grandson?"

"Yep." I nod. "Just you wait 'till you see his picture. He looks just like Terry."

CHAPTER 42

THERE'S A BIRTHDAY card lying on the mat when I come home from work on New Year's Eve. I pick it up and open it, glad of another one to share the mantelpiece with Mum's offering. I open the envelope, and there's a well-dressed woman from the 1950's sitting in an armchair reading two equally well-dressed children a story.

'And the man asked her to marry him, but she said no. She lived happily ever after, never cleaned the house, never darned any socks, and never cooked any dinners."

I laugh out loud, even though the card is from Anita. I eagerly scan the handwriting inside.

'Happy birthday, Paul. I'm off to London soon in the New Year. Here's a First Footing ticket for tonight as a birthday present. See you by the skating rink about 9.30 for old times' sake if you're free? Love from Anita. x'

I handle the ticket as though it's made out of gold dust. Never in my wildest dreams did I imagine this. I was all for going down the Rat and Pigeon and having a joke with Ray. Instead I have the wherewithal in my hands to the evening of my dreams.

I take time with my appearance like I'm going on a first date. I'm showered, powdered up and smelling like a Turkish brothel by 7pm, and spend the next 2 hours pacing around, unable to settle. I know it'll take me half an hour to walk to Princes Street, and I set off at ten to nine, eager to arrive on time or even a little early.

She's already waiting there for me. As I walk up to her I remember last New Year's Eve, shudder slightly, and make an early resolution to be on my best behaviour and treat her like Dresden china.

"Thanks for the ticket." I grin. "This beats listening to Ray moaning on all night."

Anita smiles at me.

"I thought you'd like it."

I look around. The street is starting to fill up and a band has already begun to play.

"Do you want to find a pub?"

She shakes her head and indicates towards the skating rink.

"Ever tried ice skating?"

I blanch at the idea, but keep a stiff upper lip.

"Er…no. Can't say I have."

"I've only been a few times. Come on; it'll be something different."

I step gingerly out onto the ice like a man with two wooden legs, holding on desperately to the side rail.

"It's not too bad, this…"

Anita roars with laughter and takes my hand.

"Loosen up; go with the flow!"

I enjoy the warmth that the contact brings.

"I'm going to flow along the ice on my arse in a minute, I don't know about anything else."

She's giggling for all she's worth, and it's a lovely sound. I'm happy to tit about for her benefit all night if it makes her happy. Fortunately I soon pick up the hang of it, and before long we're skating slowly round hand in hand like Torvill and Dean gone wrong, and I'm having the time of my life. Anita glances across to me.

"Having a good birthday?"

I grab both of her hands, give them a squeeze, and attempt a little whirl around.

"The best!"

My boots suddenly slide out from under me and I fall flat on my backside, but I don't care. Anita helps me up and I laugh as I brush myself off.

"I think I'm due for a drink or twelve, but actually what I really fancy is a hot chocolate to warm up."

"They're selling them over there." Anita points to a rink-side café. "You sit down and I'll get them."

I think I'm going to get a bruise on my arse. I sit down gingerly, and it's a relief to rest my feet in the heavy boots. Anita, carrying two hot chocolates, walks along the outer rubber flooring in her skates with the ease of a pro.

"Get this down you, as my mother used to say."

I take a grateful sip.

"Thanks. How *is* your mum?"

"She's fine. Dave is still trying to get her to marry him, but she doesn't want to know."

"I don't blame her." I say. "Us men are just trouble."

"Oh, I don't know…." Anita trills. "You're all grown up; I like the new you."

"Really?" I smile at her. "Keep going; I'm all ears."

We sit companionably and drink our hot chocolates. This is the first New Year's Eve since I was sixteen where so far not one drop of alcohol has touched my lips. I decide there and then that tonight, just for once, not one drop is going to either. I ask the question that's beginning to bother me somewhat.

"When will you move back in with your mum then?" Anita looks into her cup.

"In a fortnight. Julie is up to speed at work, and my job at Dodd's is soon coming to an end."

Did I detect a note of sadness in her voice? I hear my own mother's voice telling me to go and get my girl back. I reason the night is young, and that it's up to me to try and get her to change her mind.

"Once more around the rink and then we'll have a walk along Princes Street."

"Okay."

We hold hands and skate a little closer together than we were before. Soon we're in step with each other and weave slowly around little kiddies and absolute beginners with ease. Anita picks up the pace and I follow, knowing full well that I'm going to be crippled in the morning.

"Hey Christopher Dean! Look at you!"

I grin at her and grab the side rails to stop for a moment. The band in Princes Street has turned up the volume, I'm with the girl I want to be with for the rest of my life, and the world is mine for the taking. As Anita crashes to a stop beside me I cup her chin with my hands and look into her eyes.

"I love you." I tell her and mean every word. "I'm so sorry for ballsing everything up."

She doesn't say a word, but moves up close and puts her arms around my waist. It's the most wonderful feeling as I rest my chin on the top of her head. I cannot, *will* not let this moment go to waste.

"Don't go to London." I whisper in her ear. "Stay here; stay here with me. I've changed; give me a last chance. I love you so much."

"I'll think about it." Anita laughs. "But you're going to have to go all out to convince me."

I don't care about going up Castlehill to see the fireworks, and neither does Anita. As I walk along Princes Street with my girl I'm walking on air. We stay on the outside of the crowds, and eventually make our way back to the flat. I don't even bother putting the hall light on as we close the door behind us. It feels great to stand there in the dark holding Anita in my arms as midnight strikes to herald in the New Year and the new Paul Christopher McAdam.

"Happy New Year, baby. I'm so sorry that you had a miscarriage." I hold her tighter in the blackness. "It was my fault; all the stress I put you through."

There's a bit of a silence before she replies.

"There was no baby, Paul."

Stunned, I put on the hall light, tilt her chin up to me, and look down on her.

"No baby? What d'you mean?"

I hear her sigh as she tries to find the right words to speak.

"I had to get some time on my own away from you to be able to speak to the police. All I did was drink a cup of salt water to make myself sick and keep taking my pill instead of having a week's break."

In the past this would have sent me over the edge. Now I just hold her tighter to me.

"Hinny, thank God you did! Without going to prison I'd be the same old Paul McAdam, hitting out at anyone and everyone. Hopefully by my reaction now you can see I've changed?"

She nods and kisses me.

"They say prison changes some people for the worse. With you, I think going there and meeting Christine was the best thing that could have happened."

"You're wrong there." I whisper in her ear. "The best thing that's ever happened to me is *you*."

As I pick Anita up and carry her towards the bedroom I have no doubt in my mind that my 23rd birthday has been the best one I've ever had, even though I'm stone cold sober and haven't had even one pint of beer.

CHAPTER 43

I SEE 2002 rushing by, and there's one thing I can't get out of my mind and absolutely *have* to get off my chest, even though I've been sworn to secrecy. Anita can tell that something's bothering me, and she bides her time waiting for me to spill the beans. Eventually I do as she serves me up a fish finger sandwich one Saturday lunchtime. How the sight of three fish fingers in a slice of bread manages to tip me over the edge I'll never know, but hey, it does.

"Ian McAdam wasn't my real dad."

Anita puts too much tomato sauce on her sandwich in surprise. It spurts out over the bread and the rest of the table like drops of blood.

"Eh?"

She looks up at me and I hate myself for what I've got to do to Mum."

"Get ready for this. Mum had an affair when Terry was small. I'm the result. My dad was somebody called Richard Ellis, who was the manager of a care home where she worked. Paul was his middle name."

"Blimey!" Anita licks tomato sauce off her fingers. "When did you find this out?"

"On Christmas Day when I went round to Mum's. She's embarrassed; don't let on you know."

"Of course not." Anita nods. "You want to find him, don't you?"

"Does the Pope wear a dress? You bet I do, but I don't know if Mum will ever speak to me again."

"She will, don't you worry. She probably *wants* you to find him. That's why she told you."

If she isn't watching soap operas, sometimes my wife speaks a lot of sense. I suddenly consider it's my duty to find my real dad, and take my phone out of my pocket.

"I made a note of the name of the care home on here when she said it." I go into the 'Notes' section and read aloud. "Here it is; The Beeches in Elderslie Street. I think it might be in Glasgow."

Anita takes a sip of tea.

"We'll get finished up here and then we can Google it and find out where it is and what happened to the manager.

I give the phone to Anita that evening in case I say the wrong thing and balls it all up again. Anita puts the speaker on so that I can hear. Her new job in a call centre answering the phone has given her an authoritative kind of telephone voice that quite puts the wind up me.

"Good evening." Anita trills to a female voice at the other end. "Please can I speak to Richard Ellis?"

There's a silence.

"Who?"

"Mister Richard Ellis. I think he's the manager there."

"Oh, *Ricky!*" The voice apparently sees the light. "Ricky

left and went on to manage Highcross Nursing Home in Canonmills."

"Thanks."

Anita ends the call and looks at me.

"Canonmills is near here, isn't it?"

"Sure is." I nod. "Google it and give them a call, hinny. You're doing great."

She looks up the number and dials it, gives me a smile, and passes me the phone.

"You've seen how easy it is. You have a go."

I can hear it ringing at the other end. A woman answers and I feel a stab of disappointment that it's not my father's voice.

"Hi. I'd like to make an appointment to see Richard Ellis please."

"What about?"

The voice sounds bored, and in the past I'd start mouthing off and telling her to mind her own fucking business. However, it's the new me, and I count to ten.

"About finding a place for my mother."

I can hear pages of what I presume is a diary being turned over.

"He's free tomorrow afternoon at four o'clock, or Monday morning at nine thirty."

I mask a small stab of excitement at the thought of meeting up with the man who was brave enough to ignore Ian McAdam's wrath and have an affair with my mother.

"I'm at work on Monday morning, so it'll have to be tomorrow at four."

"What's your name?

I think it best not to mention a moniker that might ring warning bells too soon.

"Paul Fairfax."

"See you tomorrow then."

With a click the phone went dead. I turn to Anita open-mouthed, and she hugs me.

He's about 60 and balding, although slim and wiry like me. I can't see why Mum fancied him; he does nothing for me. However, perhaps he looked the bees' knees about 25 years ago. He smiles at me as he ushers me into his office and closes the door.

"You would like to speak to me about a place for your mother?"

I nod.

"In a way. Not about a place, but about my mother."

I look at him, and I can tell the cogs are whirring around in his head.

"My name is Paul McAdam. My mother is Molly McAdam. She used to *work* with you."

I put an emphasis on the *work*, and he catches my

drift. "Molly? You're her son?"

"Yeah, and yours too, she tells me. I thought that it was about time we met up."

He's nearly falling off his chair.

"Don't worry. Mum doesn't know I'm here. She never wanted to break up your family. She told me at Christmas. I'm doing this off my own bat."

My father looks me over and sighs.

"I never knew. She left when she was expecting you, but I assumed the baby was her husband's. Pleased to meet you, Paul." He holds out his arm. "Call me Ricky, for want of something better."

"Hi Ricky." I shake his hand and smile. "I'm glad you haven't chucked me out."

"No, no. Not at all." Ricky stares at me. "You're like your mother, you know."

"Yes, so I've been told."

"I'd very much like to meet up with Molly again if she's willing. I'm a widower; my wife died two years ago. My children are married now. I've often thought of your mother over the years and wondered where she is."

"She lives in Glasgow, and I can tell you, she's never forgotten you."

Ricky looks fit to bust.

"Give her my phone number." He scribbles on a piece of paper and gives it to me. "I'll leave it up to her of course."

"I'll give her the number." I nod at him. "Nice to meet you."

Ricky shows me to the door.

"The pleasure is all mine."

EPILOGUE- ANITA
CHAPTER 44
OCTOBER 2003

RICHARD'S CRY WAKES me from a dreamless slumber, and already my breasts are tingling. I yawn and realise that I seem to spend all of my waking hours yearning for sleep.

I turn over towards Paul, but he's not lying next to me. Smiling, I get stiffly out of bed and find my dressing gown and slippers. I know exactly where he'll be.

I pad along to the baby's room and take a peek around the door. Paul sits in the rocking chair and has Richard lying on his chest under his dressing gown. In the four weeks that we've been parents, 9 times out of 10 Paul is up and out of bed before me every night without complaint, soothing the baby before his feed. I yawn again and shake the sleep from my head.

"How long have you been sitting there?"

Paul looks up at me and smiles.

"A while. We've had a clean bum, and he's even tried rooting around my titties, but he's out of luck there I'm afraid, hence the cries. I told him that sooner or later

Mummy will be along."

He stands up and hands the baby to me as I slump into the rocking chair.

"I'll bring you a cup of tea while you do your stuff."

The whole world is asleep except Paul, Richard and me. I put the baby to my breast and he begins to suckle greedily. My eyes close as I rock the chair with my legs. I never realised in all my wildest dreams that looking after a new-born baby could be so exhausting.

Paul returns with tea and toast, and all three of us sit happily munching away. To say I'm flabbergasted at my husband's childcare skills is an understatement. Paul is going out of his way to be everything Ian McAdam was not; a hands-on helpmate to me, and a caring father to Richard. Molly's eyes light up every time she sees her grandson. She's been such a help to me in the last few months, and the birth has also brought her closer to her own son. She and Paul's real father are going to set up home together very soon. Paul is slowly getting to know his father and is absolutely over the moon about it and the fact that he now has 2 step-brothers and a step-sister, although as far as Molly's concerned I'm still not supposed to know who Ricky is. Molly eventually received a suspended sentence for failing to report Ian McAdam's murder, but so far I think has not been brave enough to tell Ricky.

My one hope for Paul is that Terry gets in touch one day. We sent details of Richard's birth to the house we stayed at, but so far have not received any reply. I realise that Terry doesn't want to be found by the police, but it would be nice for Paul just to receive a phone call or a text message from his brother. They both share the same horrific childhood that brutalised Paul and sent Terry wild. Even though they are dissimilar in looks, where Paul takes after Molly and I assume Terry looks like his dad, they seemed quite close in Sydney, and I know Paul misses him; being of the opinion that having 2 step-brothers is not quite the same.

My dad was wrong about Paul. I phoned him up and told him so a while ago, and he has conceded defeat. The two of them get along quite well now, especially when Richard came along to bridge the gap. Tricia had another little girl, and it seems weird that I have a son only a few months younger than my step-sister Charlotte.

I have come to terms with the fact that Paul murdered Catherine Taylor. He was a different person back then, and the spell in prison and the kindness of Christine Lessing gave me a man who is more like his real father. He thinks before he acts, and he's everything I could wish for in a husband. I went with him when he took flowers to Catherine's grave. The tears he cried were real, and I know he will carry the guilt of what he has done for the rest of his life.

Mum's finally given in and married Dave. I think that when Paul and I got back together it got her thinking about her own future. I'm thrilled for her, and I'm glad for myself that I gave Paul another chance. Paul and I went to Mum's wedding. I gave her a hug and reminded her that life is short, and that we should seek out and grab our chance of happiness wherever we can find it. She even invited Dad and Tricia to the wedding, and funnily enough, Dad and Dave now get on like a house on fire.

THE END

If you have enjoyed this story, you may also like 'A House Without Windows' by Stevie Turner.

"Devastating, creepy, and deeply affecting, Stevie Turner's *A House Without Windows* is many things: among them are several different, disturbing love stories, a tale of abduction, imprisonment, and menace, a narrative of a woman clinging to hope in the face of utter despair, and a portrait of the claustrophobic world of a victimized child and the tormented adult she becomes. The multiple, shifting narrators effectively portray the disorienting madness of Edwin Evans and the effects of his psychotic actions on every victim his insanity engulfs.

Definitely not for kids, but highly recommended, indeed."
- *Thom Stark*

OTHER BOOKS BY STEVIE TURNER:

THE PILATES CLASS
A HOUSE WITHOUT WINDOWS
FOR THE SAKE OF A CHILD
LILY: A SHORT STORY
NO SEX PLEASE, I'M MENOPAUSAL!
A RATHER UNUSUAL ROMANCE
THE DAUGHTER-IN-LAW SYNDROME
REVENGE
THE NOISE EFFECT: A SHORT STORY
THE DONOR
LIFE: 18 SHORT STORIES
WAITING IN THE WINGS
MIND GAMES
REPENT AT LEISURE
A NOVELLA COLLECTION
CRUISING DANGER
ALYS IN HUNGERLAND
A MARRIAGE OF CONVENIENCE

www.ingramcontent.com/pod-product-compliance
Lightning Source LLC
Chambersburg PA
CBHW070604170726
48291CB00003B/690